---- ★ ----

THERE HAD BEEN A HOMICIDE.

Through the doorway Salter could see three or four technicians working around the body. When a victim of a violent assault is discovered, the first job is to preserve life. Thus, the fire department and the ambulance team are called. After them, and in spite of them, the police must also try to preserve the scene intact. The more people who contaminate the scene, including the medics, the harder it is to isolate the evidence. In this case, Salter guessed that the emergency crews had been able to do their job almost without touching the body. Fisher lay on his back, naked except for his boxer shorts, an old military dagger sticking out of his chest.

---- ★ ----

"Well done . . . a supreme example of balanced writing."

—*Murder Ad Lib*

"Eric Wright is right on target."

—*Mostly Murder*

Also available from Worldwide Mystery by
ERIC WRIGHT

A QUESTION OF MURDER
A SENSITIVE CASE

ERIC WRIGHT
FINAL CUT

WORLDWIDE.

TORONTO • NEW YORK • LONDON
AMSTERDAM • PARIS • SYDNEY • HAMBURG
STOCKHOLM • ATHENS • TOKYO • MILAN
MADRID • WARSAW • BUDAPEST • AUCKLAND

FINAL CUT

A Worldwide Mystery/November 1992

This edition is reprinted by arrangement with Charles Scribner's Sons, an imprint of Macmillan Publishing Company.

ISBN 0-373-26107-1

Printed in U.S.A.

For Bob Rodgers

PART ONE

ONE

THE ST. LAWRENCE Market in Toronto consists of two buildings separated by Front Street.

The south building is the original market hall, and some of it dates back to the time in the nineteenth century when this was Toronto's downtown (after which the area declined for a hundred years until it was rediscovered in the 1960s). To the first-time visitor, the South Market looks dedicated to beef. Butchers to the left and right compete with those down the center in offering thousands of pounds of steaks, roasts, ground beef, and stewing beef, all cheap, and cheaper still if you buy in bulk. There is other meat around—several tons of chickens and pork chops are on sale, and a few hundred legs of lamb—but beef is the serious meat.

After a while, the visitor begins to see around the mountains of meat and notices that the building also houses (at the back) some of Toronto's best fishmongers and (tucked into the sides and the corners) three very good cheese stalls. Below, in the basement, the emphasis is not so much on bulk as on variety. Here you can buy twenty-eight different kinds of rice and an endless assortment of beans as well as coffee and olives and cabbage rolls and dried mushrooms.

The South Market is open every day except for Sundays and Mondays, although it does most of its business on Saturdays.

The North Market, across the street, sometimes known as the Farmers' Market, is only open on Saturdays from 5:00 A.M. The stalls are temporary, rented for the day by farmers, butchers, and bakers from out of town who bring in fresh eggs, real bread, naturally raised meat and poultry, and a superb variety of sausages—German, Ukrainian, Argentinian, Italian, and even a bland imitation of English "bangers." Many of the vendors have sold out by two o'clock, and serious shoppers come early to get their pick and to avoid the ten o'clock crush of tourists and locals having a day out.

At six o'clock on a Saturday morning, the whole market is busy; by seven it is full, and it stays jammed until after lunch.

On this day, a tall, erect, gray-haired man in his late seventies, dressed in immaculate Saturday morning clothes—a beautifully pressed khaki shirt, narrow-cuffed biscuit-colored slacks, suede shoes—emerged from the door of the North Market at the same time as another man in his thirties, a dark, curly-haired man, came through the door of the South Market. The two men passed each other in the middle of Front Street, bumped slightly, apologized, then went on their way. When the younger man reached the door of the North Market, he stopped, turned, and looked back at the old man, now disappearing through the door opposite. The young man watched him go for a few moments, then started to recross the street in pursuit, slowly at first, then running as he reached the door.

By the time he was inside the south building, his quarry was well down the aisle, and the young man pushed and jostled his way forward through the crowds, nearly catching his man at Alex's cheese stall, then losing him as a passing acquaintance grabbed his arm to chat. Shaking off his friend, the young man raced down the east aisle, then came back and began to run down the other aisle, jumping to see above the heads of the shoppers as he looked for the old man.

At this point, a third man ran out of the crowd of onlookers, shouting, "What the hell is going on?" and grabbed the young man's arm.

The young man stopped, looked pointedly at the hand on his sleeve, and said, irritably, "Somebody take this clown away," whereupon the third man launched himself at the young man, clawing and swinging and screaming.

The young man tried to hold his attacker at arm's length, but it was inevitable that if he scrabbled long enough the third man would connect, and when he did, his loosely bunched hand caught the curly-haired man on the ear, hurting him not at all but causing him finally to react by grabbing his attacker by the throat and throwing him at Mike's fish stall, scattering a display of Atlantic salmon.

Staff Inspector Charlie Salter of the Metropolitan Police congratulated himself on his control. A policeman's first instinct is to unpick fighters, but Salter's better instinct told him that the young man was in no danger from his assailant, who was noisy and furious but not otherwise very alarming, and there were guards, off-duty policemen, twenty years younger than Salter, whose job it was to deal with problems like this.

Now a fourth man arrived, talking as he approached the scuffling pair. "Not on the set, Stanley, I told you. Not on the set. Now, get out of the building and go wait for me somewhere. In the commissary truck. You listening?"

"What the hell is going on?" the third man, Stanley, screamed again. "Diamond is supposed to ask the cheese guy if he knows who Vigor is. The cheese guy knows him, for Christ's sake. He's an old customer."

"I cut that out," the curly-haired man said.

"*You* cut it out! The scene is crucial." Stanley was nearly crying with rage.

"It doesn't work. I'm chasing the guy. I don't stop to ask the cheese man the way. I go after him. It's not in the character to talk to the cheese guy."

"It's goddamn *essential*."

"It's phony. You'll have to put the clue in some other way."

Stanley gathered himself for another assault, and Charlie Salter got ready. As the man began his run, Salter stuck out his foot and, grabbing him by his upper sleeve at the same time, pulled hard, swinging him around and bringing him to his knees. At that point, two uniformed policemen decided they had a role to play and took charge of the kneeling man, and Salter let go.

The fourth man now said something to the curly-haired actor, who nodded and walked away, and Stanley got to his feet. The fourth man spoke to the two policemen. "Take this guy to the commissary truck and keep him there."

As the guards hoisted him up, Stanley sagged in defeat, and Salter saw that he had never entirely lost control, that some part of his anger had been assumed for effect. Now the man abruptly stopped protesting. "I quit," he said. "You hear? I quit. Tell these guys to take their hands off me." He shrugged his disarrayed jacket back onto his shoulders. "Okay, I'll wait in the truck, Crabtree. Before I leave, I want a few minutes to explain to you what a goddamn dog's breakfast Diamond and this guy''—indicating a fifth man—''and you are making of my script. No wonder you guys are the laughingstock of the world.''

He walked away with an exaggerated swagger, and Crabtree nodded to the guards to follow.

Crabtree said to the fifth man, ''Let's try it again.''

In his turn, the fifth man said something to an assistant, and the crew began to set up once more.

Salter went back to his coffee and settled back to watch. He was on assignment, and this was his first day on the job; it looked like an interesting one.

TWO

HE HAD BEEN briefed three days earlier by his former boss, Staff Superintendent Orliff, now retired.

For the last year, Orliff had been dividing his time between building a cottage in the Kawartha Hills and acting as adviser to any film company that wanted to make a movie involving police work in Toronto. It made for a pleasant rhythm in his life and a nice supplement to his pension. Toronto had long since been discovered by Hollywood as an ideal location to imitate a medium-sized law-abiding American city, especially if the movie was set in the gentler past. But if a story was actually set in Toronto, then someone was needed to keep the howlers out of the script. In the first instance, Orliff's job was to eliminate all references to the ranks of captain, lieutenant, and patrolman, none of which exist in the Toronto police, and to keep an eye out for any other Americanizations of Canadian culture, changing back sodas to soft drinks and miles to kilometers, for example. In this latest job he had run into another kind of problem, which he was no longer licensed to deal with. Salter's boss, the deputy chief, had then had the bright idea of sending Salter in to investigate, under the guise of taking over Orliff's role as adviser.

The two men met in Salter's office.

"How did it start?" Salter asked.

"The first thing was the fire alarm. Right in the middle of a scene they were shooting in Rosedale one night, three trucks and two ambulances came scream-ing in. Someone had turned in an alarm. Then there was the police call. That could've been a public-spirited citizen.'' Orliff laughed. "They were filming the leading actor breaking into an office downtown, and the holdup squad arrived to stop them. Very ef-ficient we looked. Not just the plainclothes squad but about six patrol cars, all with lights and sirens.''

"A joker?''

"Could be, sure. That's what I told them. Then, the next day, this guy Henry Vigor, the villain in the movie, was picked up from his hotel and taken down to Niagara Falls for some background shots that weren't in the script. They thought he'd been kid-napped. He had been, in a way.''

"How did they do that? Someone impersonate his driver?''

"Easier than that.'' Orliff hitched his chair for-ward, leaned toward Salter, and lifted a hand to indi-cate that he did not wish to be interrupted for the next few sentences. "See, the limousines that take the leading actors around are all under the control of one guy, the transportation coordinator. Every day he gets his orders for the next day about where and when to have the cars ready, and he tells the drivers. Now this day, very late, he got a call from someone calling himself the producer's assistant, changing the time that Vigor had to be picked up the following morn-ing. Vigor has his own driver, so the coordinator told him about the change. Vigor got a call, too, telling him to be ready half an hour early. So his driver appeared the next morning, and off they went to Horseshoe Falls. There wasn't anyone around, of course, but they stayed where they were, and by the time the driver phoned in to find out what was going on, they'd used up half the morning."

Salter waited. There was more to come.

"So it might still be a joker," Orliff continued. "But it's someone working on the film, someone who knows the routines. Then, last week again, while the hero was doing this scene inside the office, all the sprinklers came on. If it is a joker, he's very persistent, and it's costing a lot of money." Orliff leaned back. "You like it here, Charlie?"

Salter looked up, startled. His office was in the new police building on College Street. Orliff's question could refer to the particular room Salter had been assigned, to the building, or, conceivably, to the police force, though this last was unlikely unless Orliff was preparing to tell Salter about another job he had heard of, more glamorous, for twice the pay. Then Salter remembered that Orliff had retired from the old Jarvis Street building. He had never worked in the new building. "Here" was the building on College Street.

"Once you're at work, it's all the same," Salter said. "But for the first little while I felt as if I was on stage, being a cop for the tourists in the foyer, sorry, atrium."

"What?"

"Atrium." Salter opened a drawer and took out a brochure. "'A central atrium rises twelve stories, offering daylight to the interior,'" he read.

Orliff nodded. "They go from one extreme to the other. Up on Eglinton, 53 Division has that building with all the little slits in the walls, which makes it look like a Foreign Legion outpost, where they hang up the suspects on hooks in the basement, but this place is like a jungle gym for adults."

"It's postmodern," Salter said. "It was in the paper last week."

"Yeah? You guys should be carrying ray guns, then."

Salter smiled. "I'll show you around when we're through."

Orliff nodded. "Where were we?"

"You told me what's been happening. What do we know?"

Orliff felt in the pockets of his jacket and pulled out several folded sheets of paper. He was wearing an open-necked, checked cotton shirt and a madras jacket to cope with the early June heat wave. Salter realized that this was the first time he had ever seen Orliff in anything but a blue suit. Even the suntan looked strange.

Orliff unfolded the sheaf of notes. "I did a little work, just to get you started. All the alarm calls were put in by a man—ordinary voice, slight European accent. Our dispatcher thought he sounded German, but nobody else could identify him. Half the people on the set have got some kind of accent. I've got a list of the ones who couldn't have turned on that sprinkler. It's just about everyone who was involved in the scene." Orliff slid a sheet of paper across Salter's desk.

"What's the movie about?"

"It's a thriller. Story of a guy who is tracking down a war criminal. This guy—the hero in the movie—his father was in a concentration camp, and somehow he has kept a picture of one of the SS guards who was responsible for executing prisoners. The old man is dead now, but before he died, he swore he saw this guard in Toronto, getting on a subway train, or some such. His son still has the picture, and he's dedicated himself to finding the guy. The son has even got an expert to age the face in the picture to show what he might look like today. Then one day he sees him, and the chase starts.

"He's down shopping one Saturday morning at the St. Lawrence Market, and they pass each other as the hero is crossing from the South Market to the North Market—you know, across Front Street from one building to the other. Then he loses him in the crowd, but now he's as sure as his father was, so he goes down to the market every Saturday morning and watches at the crossing. Then he sees the guy and follows him home, checks up on him, and sure enough, it's the right man.

"It sounds a little farfetched to me—the way he catches up with him, I mean—but it's a thriller, the kind where you don't ask too many questions as long as something's happening. It starts out very quiet, with the story of the hero and his father, and then lots of short scenes showing you the hero, who's a lawyer working with this Jewish group who spend their time looking for war criminals. All of this is just to show you how dedicated he is, because they're no help to him. All the time, the hero keeps the picture of this Nazi on his desk. His wife is always pleading with him to forget the whole thing, but he won't. Then he sees the guy, and off we go."

"Why are they making it here? Is it cheaper in Toronto?"

"Yeah, but that's not the point. This is a very Canadian movie. Lots of shots of the subway and the CN Tower, stuff like that. And it all ends up in a chase scene down at Harbourfront. Then a big shoot-out on

Lake Ontario. That qualifies them for a subsidy from the government.''

Salter said, ''You had any thoughts about who the joker might be and what he's after?''

''There are lots of possibilities. I'd go for the personal first. Someone with a grudge against the movie—or someone in the movie—and wants to screw it up.''

''You picked up on anything like that?''

''It's unbelievable.'' Orliff spread out a hand and ticked the points off his fingers, grinning. ''First there's the writer. It's his script, and he thinks the director is an asshole and that the leading actor, the hero, is useless, and he says so, too. So naturally they don't like him. Then the director and the hero don't get along. Then there's a difference of opinion as to whether the hero is the lead or the villain is. Both the actors have contracts giving them some kind of special rights. Those are just the main ones. Pretty well everyone has been in a shouting match with everyone else. Except for the old guy, Henry Vigor. He's here to pick up a paycheck and get back home to England as soon as possible. I kinda like him. He seems like a real pro. You'd never know he was an actor.''

Orliff was looking around the office again, apparently losing interest in what he was saying. Salter needed to pump him dry before he disappeared. ''None of these people would want the film wrecked, would they?''

''You wouldn't think so, would you? I'm just telling you what to expect, though. No, if this is serious—and it may be—you're looking for someone who wants the film stopped, but all of the people I've mentioned must have an interest in finishing it.''

''What's the damage so far?''

"Four days of shooting." Orliff put the folded notes back in his pocket. "The budget calls for thirty-five days of shooting, and they are using them up too fast. They can't afford four days. I don't understand all of it. Bad weather doesn't cost them so much if they don't shoot at all, and they've got some kind of insurance, but this type of waste costs a lot of money because everybody has to be paid and they get nothing on film.

"Then there's somebody called the guarantor. Everyone seems to be afraid of him, because if they go over budget, he can take over the whole thing. It's all money. You'll see."

Salter didn't take any notes. None of this would mean much until he met the people. "What about you?" he asked now. "Where are you going?"

"Me?" Orliff looked surprised. "I'm up to the cottage. The roof is on, the stove's working, and the bass season opens on Saturday. I have it written into my contract, like these movie actors, Diamond and Vigor." He grinned. "Besides, this needs an investigator. I'm retired. Be a nice job for you. What the center was set up for."

Salter nodded. Ostensibly, the Special Affairs Center had been created to take care of the unusual, whatever didn't fit into the regular work of the different departments, and it had survived because of some early successes and through Orliff's skill at not making enemies. In fact, Orliff had created the center himself out of a number of different needs: There was the administrative need of his boss, the deputy chief, to have a place in his budget where he could store a little money, to have an item that could not be too closely scrutinized; there was Orliff's desire to be in charge of something quiet, away from the regular line of administrative duties; finally, there was the need to create something big enough so that Orliff could stay in the office while Salter went out on assignments.

Now Salter was in charge, and the center had long established its usefulness to the deputy chief. The only danger for Salter lay in being envied and resented for seeming to be on a permanent, slightly glamorous special assignment. But when he got the job, he was old enough and experienced enough to be aware of the danger, and he had always been very careful not to step on the toes of anyone in the regular units—the homicide squad, for example, into whose territory he had strayed several times—and over seven years he had built up a good working relationship with all the units he came into contact with. He also didn't look the part of a hotshot special investigator. He was fifty-four, of medium build, with scanty brown hair and a lack of distinguishing facial characteristics. He habitually wore a tweed jacket and gray pants, a white shirt, and a blue tie with red geese, unless the tie was being cleaned, when he wore a blue tie decorated with red fishhooks. He played squash frequently, and badly, with all the enthusiasm of a late convert, so he was in fair physical condition, but he needed glasses for close work.

"Will you be available if I want to talk?" he asked.

"Sure. Bring your rod." Orliff started to get up.

"Hold on. What are the other possibilities?"

"Oh, yeah." Orliff looked at his watch. "Is there a canteen? I need some coffee."

"I'll get some sent in. Homicide is putting on one of their seminars, and the canteen will be full of your old pals."

"Don't bother, then. Let's walk over to Fran's after. You can show me the building on the way." Orliff sank back in his chair. "What else? Right. The movie is about war criminals. There's a very slight possibility that the film is making someone uncomfortable. According to the writer, there are still lots of Nazis in Canada. If he's right, and there must be a few, then maybe one of them doesn't like the sound of this movie."

"He'd still have to have someone on the set, wouldn't he?"

"That's what I mean. It's remote. Just a possibility. But I can't really see this film bothering anyone. Still, I mentioned it to the investigating sergeant, and I think he passed it on to Intelligence. Ask Parker. More likely is another possibility. Some kind of right-wing mob, the 'Keep Canada Pure' gang, maybe. There's one little gang who demonstrate. The leader is a pervert. I mean, he gets his kicks out of dressing up as a storm trooper. Two of his lieutenants, as he calls them, are like him, but not so bright, and the rest are just goons he pays to come to the meetings. Intelligence knows all about him, but they don't think he's in town. But if it's not him, then it might be someone like him who could be dangerous, a lunatic on a mission."

"What's the security?"

"They've got a company guarding the production offices and patrolling the permanent sets, and they've hired six of our off-duty men to help out."

Salter waited to see if Orliff had any more to add.

Orliff, apparently sensing some misgivings on Salter's part, continued.

"It's interesting as hell. You wouldn't believe how long it takes them to shoot a scene of two guys shaking hands. Especially with this one actor, Diamond. He wants to know what's going on underneath, all the time. He calls it the subtext. But the other guy, the villain, he just wants to know how they want it. He does the old-pro bit. You know, 'I can shake hands in six different ways,' he says. 'Which one do you want?' No one will take any notice of you. You'll soon melt into the woodwork. Except for the producer, everyone will think you're just a replacement for me, an old fart hired to make sure they don't write any *Hill Street Blues* stuff into the script."

Salter said, "Let's get some coffee."

The two men put on their jackets and walked out to the foyer. Before they took the elevator down, Salter showed Orliff the view from the interior balcony down to the courtyard below, the atrium.

"Marinelli said it reminds him of a Neapolitan slum," Salter said. Marinelli was a sergeant on the gambling squad. "He meant it as a compliment."

"Maybe it's supposed to."

They walked down the long ramp to College Street, then began to circle the building, walking first along Bay Street.

Orliff said, "Weird color, isn't it? Is the whole thing made of stone?"

"They're all that color now, all the new hotels and apartment blocks. Liver and blue. Haven't you noticed?"

They looked at the building together. Salter read from his brochure. "The building is clad in salmon-colored granite, making it warm and approachable."

"What the hell is that?" Orliff pointed to a bronze figure of a child pulling a cart. On the cart was an obelisk, about twenty feet high, engraved with the police motto To Serve and Protect.

Salter consulted his brochure. "He represents the community. That stone thing represents authority. That guy"—Salter pointed along the street to a male figure carrying blocks of stone on his shoulders—"is bringing the law. These two are working together with the police to build their community, it says here."

"What about her?" Orliff asked, pointing to a bronze of a female police officer with a trowel in her hand. "Oh, the hell with it. Let's have some coffee."

When they were settled in Fran's, Salter asked, "What's happening on the set at the moment?"

"Nothing. See, the old guy who's playing the villain has got to rest up for a day. It's in his contract that he has to have a day off after so many working days, so they schedule with that in mind. The crew works a five-day week—it's all unionized—though they can do a sixth day on overtime. So today and tomorrow are like the sixth and seventh days after the five working days. Nothing is scheduled, and the chiefs are all having conferences."

Salter considered. The trouble sounded more like spite than a real threat, and whoever was causing it could well be satisfied already. It was probably a baby-sitting job, but watching a movie being made seemed like a good way to spend a week or two, and if the deputy chief had nothing more urgent he wanted done, then Salter had better go along with it. He repeated his question. "Who else will know that I'm on the job?"

"Only the producer. Some of the uniformed guys will recognize you, but they'll think you're just advising, unless you need them, of course. The idea is, the producer wants everyone to think the trouble's over. But he wants us—you—to sniff around. The deputy agrees it's the best—and the cheapest—way to handle it. We've had each incident officially investigated. You can read the reports."

Salter tried to think it through quickly. "I might need some help. Someone undercover."

"What for?"

"Because everyone will clam up around me, even though I'm supposed to be just advising. But while they're avoiding me, they might just show their hand to someone who is really undercover."

"The deputy won't buy that."

"Sure he will. It won't cost him. The film company is paying six of our guys now. Make it seven."

Orliff looked at him admiringly. "You've learned a lot. Ask Crabtree, the producer. It's mostly his money, I think." He looked through the window of the restaurant at the sky. "Don't forget. When you come up, bring your rod. There's some nice smallmouth bass in the lake."

Out on College Street, Orliff said, "There's a guy coming to town in the next few days, fella named Simple, a scriptwriter. I got to know him on the last film, and I promised him a bit of fishing in the Kawarthas." Orliff smiled. "He thinks that's the north. He's from California. If he comes looking for me, have him call my wife, would you? I'm staying up there now, but she's still in town. She'll know how to get a message up to me."

BACK IN HIS OFFICE, Salter put a call through to Staff Sergeant Wayne Mahler, in charge of the drug squad.

"Constable Ranovic," he began. "He still work for you?"

"You could call it that," the staff sergeant responded.

"What's the matter with him?"

"He's pining, that's his problem. Ever since he got spotted on that job he did for you, he's been no good for undercover stuff, so we've got him on street detail. It's honest work, but he doesn't enjoy it."

"How would you like to lose him for a couple of weeks?"

"Don't matter no mind to me. You got something glamorous for him? He'd like that."

"Keep it to yourself, will you, Wayne? I don't know if I can fix it yet."

"What's up?"

"I might need a guy to imitate an actor."

There was a long pause. "You mean someone who would walk around so that people on Yonge Street would say, I bet he's an actor? Got you. Ranovic's your boy. Let me know when I can tell him. He's free anytime."

Ranovic. A young undercover cop in the process of creating himself who spent a good deal of time looking for role models. But he had an inquiring personality, which fit the assignment. Salter picked up the phone to get the deputy's permission to approach the film company about hiring Ranovic.

AT HOME, Salter explained his assignment to Annie, his wife.

"What a lovely job. Can you get me a part?" she responded.

Salter said, "What can you do? Let's see your legs."

Annie stood up and lifted her skirt to her knees.

"Higher," Salter commanded. "Not bad. Can you dance?"

"The man said this was a thriller."

"You'd be the love interest. You mind doing nude scenes?"

"Depends. Who with?"

Salter scratched his head. The joke was running down. "Me," he said, and meant it.

Annie had no difficulty stirring Salter. Her hair was host to plenty of gray, but she had kept the complexion she had brought with her from the Maritimes, and her figure, like her legs, was better than not bad.

"Maybe you can get Seth on to the set," she said. "He'd love that."

Seth was their sixteen-year-old son.

"This isn't *Swan Lake*. It's a thriller about war criminals."

"That sounds like a crack."

"All I'm saying is that there's no connection between hunting Nazis and learning a pas de deux."

"It shows what's in your head. All *I* meant is that Seth might just be interested in seeing how films get made. If he were apprenticed to a carpenter, you wouldn't be so edgy."

It was true. Three months before, Seth, as a result of being given a tiny part in a school production of *A Midsummer Night's Dream*, a part that had involved a good deal of leaping about the stage, had become stagestruck. Then Seth's girlfriend, who attended an expensive private girls' school, had appealed to him to find two boys to lift her dance class about the stage during their annual production. When Seth persuaded a pal to join him, the teacher became ambitious and changed the program, and now the two boys had been rehearsing three hours a night for the last three months, and Seth had recently announced that he wanted to study ballet.

Annie had reacted immediately in ideal parent fashion in favor of letting him try it, a response that Salter felt was prompted by his own reaction of confusion and by her assumption of what lay behind Salter's hesitancy; but Salter's doubts, he told himself, were reasonable enough in view of the popular or police headquarters' conception of male dancers, and it was therefore ridiculous to expect him to respond with an unthinking yea, wasn't it? And wasn't her own reaction as knee jerking in its way as she assumed his was, a conditioned response, an automatic assumption that creativity or any sign of it was a good thing, no matter how trivial or self-indulgent it looked? Ever since, they had hardly mentioned it, while every night Seth came home exhausted and appeared at breakfast every morning moving as though he had arthritis.

Salter told himself he had asked all the questions a responsible parent ought. "What about school?" he had asked.

"They have tutors."

"Isn't he a little young?" Salter's experience of ballet consisted of two-second glimpses as he rotated the television dial, looking for something funny to watch.

"He *may* be too old. They like to start training them much younger."

Salter shut up, unable in his ignorance to think of a single other fact about the world of ballet that might present problems.

Seth's brother, Angus, now enrolled in the commerce program of the University of Western Ontario, said, "Jesus, Seth, you'll be poor for the rest of your life," which put Salter's teeth on edge, even though, or perhaps because, it echoed some small part of his own unease.

It took Salter's father to lay the question on the table. The old man was a retired maintenance mechanic for the Toronto Transit Commission. He was aggressively working class and wary of his son's family because Annie came from several rungs up the class ladder. Seth, however, had been a favorite of his ever since the boy had recorded his grandfather's oral history, and the old man was now inclined to sentences like "Me and Seth don't think so, do we, son?" constructing a private world of understanding between him and his grandson that Salter was too thick to enter. Now he called Salter and asked what was going on.

"Seth wants to become a ballet dancer," Salter said, his eye on Annie, who was watching and listening.

"Bloody hell. All those poofs? Does he know what's what?"

Salter searched for a sentence that would mean nothing to Annie. "I think he knows what's what, Dad."

"You sure?"

"You can tell him yourself, if you like."

"I will. I intend to. There's probably not much to worry about, though, is there? I mean, old Seth, he's a pretty *homely* lad, isn't he? But I'll talk to him. Is he there now?"

"No, he practices every night. Shall I tell him to call you?"

"No, ask him to come by. I haven't seen him for a couple of weeks. Everybody well? She all right?" This last was in reference to Annie.

"Everybody's fine. I'll tell Seth."

Salter put the phone down and looked at Annie. "My father sends his regards and has undertaken to explain to Seth what a poof is. He'd never forgive himself if Seth went uninstructed into the big, bad world of *The Nutcracker*. He doesn't think there's much to worry about, though, because Seth's so ugly no one will fancy him."

"For God's sake," Annie began, but Salter, a thought ahead, patted her on the arm.

"Leave them alone. Let Seth get on with it. He told us once, it's *his* grandfather. Remember?"

Annie laughed. "Right. We can't go on protecting the boys forever. They have to find out about your father sometime." She added, "Seth would love it, and I wouldn't mind, myself. I'd like to talk to whoever does the props."

Annie had just quit her job in a television commercials' production house. She had been responsible for props, a job she enjoyed, but she had not much liked the world of the studio, and she wanted to set up her own company, handling props for small studios on a free-lance basis.

Salter said, "Let me get my feet under the table. Then I'll introduce the whole gang of you."

THREE

THE OFFICES OF Balmuto Productions were on Sherbourne Street.

Before he heard the address, Salter had a vague expectation that he would be held up by three layers of secretaries until he finally gained access to someone in riding boots and a silk shirt holding a megaphone, but anyone dressed like that on the corner of Sherbourne and Gerrard would be surrounded by panhandlers before he got out of his car. Real despair is two blocks south on the streets surrounding the Salvation Army hostel, but the land of the homeless stretches all the way up to Gerrard Street.

Balmuto Productions shared space in an old fire station with a number of other organizations. There were five names listed by the front door, including two graphic artists and something called Rent-a-Clown. The film company was on the second floor. Salter climbed the stairs to a landing with a bare wooden floor. At one end was the open door of a copy shop; at the other, a sign on a door proclaimed Balmuto Productions. Underneath, a smaller, handwritten note read Knock and Enter. Salter did as he was told and found himself in an office that looked as if it might be the upstairs quarters of a muffler repair shop.

There was one large room with a smaller room, not much bigger than a large closet, opening off it. This smaller room was lined with cans of film stacked on shelves. A secretary worked in a tiny corner of the main room in an area fenced off like a playpen. When Salter told her his name, she indicated with a twist of her head two men sitting on a couch at the far end of the room.

As Salter opened the catch on the little gate across the doorway, one of the two men stood up and walked over to Salter with his hand extended. "Jack Crabtree," he said. "The producer."

Crabtree was a big man wearing a check shirt and khaki pants and Greb boots. He adjusted his horn-rimmed glasses to get Salter in focus and pushed a hank of flat, colorless hair off his brow. His hands were huge and hard. Salter would have guessed him to be an accountant who had retired early to run a marina.

Crabtree pulled Salter toward the couch. "This is Stanley Fisher, our scriptwriter. Charlie Salter. Charlie's taking over from Fred Orliff as adviser."

Fisher offered Salter a long, thin hand, lifting himself three inches off the couch. A delicately boned man in his late thirties: His black-and-gray hair looked sculpted in curls around his skull. "You read the script?" he asked.

Salter nodded. "Last night."

"See any problems?"

"I think you want to be careful about the color of the police cars. We're just changing over from the old yellow ones to red, white, and blue. If you use yellow cars, by the time this is released it could be slightly dated." Salter felt proud of having foreseen this problem, but Fisher was barely listening.

"There aren't any colored cars in the script," he said. "I just write 'cars.' Colors is someone else's worry. How'd the dialogue sound?"

"Cops talk like that. Sometimes. Even in Toronto."

"Goddamn right they do." Fisher turned to Crabtree. "The dialogue is the best I've done, Jack, and I'm not having some asshole actor rewrite it for me. Okay?"

Salter sat down on an old red leatherette armchair across the room from the couch, out of range of the argument he had interrupted.

"Be with you in a second, Charlie," Crabtree said, and turned back to Fisher. "We're nearly there, Stanley. We're three-quarters done. Be with you in a second, Charlie," he said again.

Fisher turned now to Salter. "Listen to this. 'He was my father. He was a witness to your crimes, and now I am his witness. I promised him that, Hauser. I'm carrying his testimony.' Got that?" Fisher asked Salter. "Now listen to what this creep changed it to. 'I'm going to get you, Hauser. I promised my daddy on his deathbed.' Do-de-do-de-do, for Christ's sake."

To Salter's relief, Fisher didn't wait for him to confirm which was the better line, but turned back to Crabtree. "I warn you, Jake. If he does it again, I'm gonna blow this thing out of the water."

"He's got the right to say the line doesn't work, Stanley."

"It's my goddamn script! Who is he, anyway? A bit player in a soap, for God's sake."

"It wasn't a soap, Stanley. It was a prime-time series, and he was a lead player. That's why we had to have him. There's no money without him."

"One more change. That's all. One more and I'll walk." He got up, drained a cup of coffee, and grabbed the script from where he had thrown it on the couch. "I'll see you in the market."

The producer let him get to the secretary's desk before he replied, softly and clearly. "I'm going to finish this picture with you or without you, Stanley. I can't finish it without him."

"Meaning?" Fisher seemed to be acting a little. He rested both palms on the secretary's desk and looked back at Crabtree over his shoulder.

Crabtree picked up his copy of the script and started to leaf through it. "Means what it says. You're going to have to change every line if necessary. Or someone is." He spoke now in an orderly, brisk voice, relaying information without looking at Fisher.

"That's it," Fisher screamed. "Take my name off this garbage." He threw his script on the floor. "You hear? You people up here know fuck-all about this business. I'm one of the hottest writers in L.A., and you don't even know that."

"I know I've got a picture to finish, and that's all I care about. So stay off the set tomorrow, Stanley. I'll protect your lines if I think I should."

"You can't keep me off the set. No way."

"Yes, I can. All right, come and listen. But if you say one word, except to me, I'll have you banned for good. I can't afford any more wasted time."

Fisher picked up his script, started to say something, then contented himself with wagging his finger at Crabtree as he backed through the gate and out the door, leaving it open.

Crabtree closed the door and came back into the room. He gave Salter a smile, a grimace, acknowledging that they had both witnessed an embarrassing scene, and sat down.

"That's the writer," Crabtree said. "As well as him I've got the lead actor, Paul Diamond, who doesn't like the lines he's been given. Then there's the actor playing the villain, Henry Vigor. He and Diamond don't get along. Vigor also thinks Fisher is a lousy writer. None of them think I know what I'm doing."

"What was that 'do-de-do' stuff about?"

"Fisher was making fun of Diamond's alliteration. I should've told him, Shakespeare did the same thing. Listen to this: 'Our eldest daughters have fordone themselves and desperately are dead.' Everybody can have an off day, except Fisher, of course. Coffee?"

"Thanks. Fisher is American, and Vigor is British. Don't we have any Canadians that could do it?"

"Don't you start. Sure we do." He paused. "Henry Vigor is Romanian, I think. Naturalized British, though. British enough to play Shakespeare at the National Theatre. Actually, Fisher is a Canadian who is making it in L.A. So is Diamond. That's why they don't trust each other's work. Everybody thinks Canadian filmmakers are second-rate. Expatriate Canadians *know* it." Crabtree smiled. "Fisher and Diamond and Vigor are names. You have to have names to get money. You have to have money to make films. But you need money from the government as well as from the dentists, and to get money from Telefilm Canada—that's the government, essentially—you have to use a certain proportion of Canadians. Fisher and Diamond qualify for that, too, so they become very important." Crabtree looked at Salter with the air of a man who knows he is talking about never-never land.

Salter said, "I've seen a lot of Vigor's movies, but I've never heard of the others."

"Don't say that aloud on the set, will you? But none of this is your problem. You want to know about this funny business."

Salter took a small notebook out of his pocket. "I got some of it from Orliff. There was a false fire alarm and a police call. And someone sent an actor to Niagara Falls. And the sprinkler. That it?"

"So far. And I can't afford much more."

"Orliff said it was costing you a lot of money."

Crabtree said, "Money and time." He lifted his hands, opening them in a pleading gesture. "Anywhere else it would be peanuts, but a hundred thousand dollars could finish me. I haven't got it." Crabtree's voice was tight and angry.

"You're nearly finished, Orliff said."

"I'm nearly *not* finished, and if I can't complete on schedule, they'll take the picture away from me."

"Who's they?"

"The dentists. The backers. They insure themselves, though, so it's really the insurance company."

Salter felt slightly dizzy with the amount of condensed information he was getting and decided to hold his questions on this, accepting that Crabtree was facing disaster.

"But you must be insured yourself, against accidents like the sprinklers?"

Crabtree nodded. "I'm insured, but it's like any other kind of insurance. When the dust settles and they've paid you off, you're still worse off."

"But you *are* close to finishing?"

"Finishing what? The shooting? We've shot about three-quarters of it. We were scheduled to shoot it in thirty-five days, and I've got enough left. Another pressure is that Henry Vigor, the villain, has other commitments, and it's in his contract that his other commitments override his commitment to us. So I'm trying to get his scenes done; then I can do some of the earlier stuff he's not in. You know anything about this business?''

Salter shook his head.

"It's time and money," Crabtree said. "Every one of these incidents wasted shooting time that was paid for.''

"What's happening today? You got a few minutes to go over the situation with me now?''

"We're not shooting today. I have to bring them together this afternoon over that script problem you were listening to. Let's go somewhere else and talk. We'll be interrupted all the time if we stay here." He turned to his secretary. "Fay, we're going down to the coffee shop. We'll be back in an hour.''

He led the way downstairs and along the street to a café plastered with Breakfast Special signs. They took a booth in the corner and ordered more coffee.

When the coffee arrived, Salter asked, "Could this be personal? I mean, have you made any enemies lately?''

"Sure. Everybody in the business who didn't get an agency grant when I did." Crabtree smiled. "No, I'm not into any feuds. I haven't screwed anybody that I know of, or anybody's wife.''

"You didn't fire some actor or not hire one who thought he should get a part, something like that?''

"No, I haven't fired anybody or broken any promises. The movie only has three real parts, including the hero's wife, who doesn't do much, but you've got to have a bit of sex, and she was cast, like Diamond and Vigor, as part of the deal with the dentists and the agencies. Fisher wanted us to get Meryl or Cher. He kept saying, 'Let's try for Meryl or Cher,' until I convinced him that if I could afford Meryl or Cher, then I could afford Dustin, too, but we're not playing in that league.'' Crabtree enunciated these famous first names to make it clear that he was quoting Fisher, not name-dropping on his own account. ''So we didn't have auditions for those parts. Three or four other small roles are played by people I had in mind from the beginning, and I got everyone I wanted. The casting director came up with the rest.''

''What about the others? The writer, cameraman, people like that?''

''Okay. One thing I didn't say is that the film is Fisher's idea in the first place. He won't get all his pay for writing the script right away like a hired hand, and he's even put a bit of his own money into it. He brought the script to me, and I put the production together. At first he wanted to be coproducer, but I managed to avoid that. That's why I've been putting up with a little bit more hassle from him than I normally would from a writer. What you walked in on this morning was me telling him to get back in his cage, that from now on he's a scriptwriter and I can have him banned from the set. The director and the director of photography are mine. We've worked together before. Apart from them there's just the first A.D.''

''What's that? Would you write down the names of these people and their jobs?''

''Sure.'' Crabtree looked around for some paper, then turned over his paper place mat. ''Writer: Fisher,'' he intoned. ''Bill Connor: director. Josef Hodek: director of photography. Tom Sherriff: first assistant director. He's the on-set organizer. I was stuck without one. This guy's a flake, but he's good in a lot of ways, and anyway, I didn't have a choice. Everyone's making movies in Toronto this summer, and there just wasn't an experienced first A.D. around. He drives me nuts because I'm never certain he's on the job. Imagine you are producing a play and on the first night you're driving down to the theater and you pass a restaurant and there's your stage manager having dinner with a blonde an hour before the curtain goes up. That's Sheriff. He's my stage manager, and I'm looking forward to firing him.''

Salter said, ''I'm going to have to find out something about how a film works. I've got to try to figure out who could have caused these incidents, what they would have to know, like when a particular scene was being made, and what access they had to have to the set. The phone calls to the police and fire departments could have been done by anyone who knew where you would be that day, even an outsider; but this sprinkler, it must have been turned on by someone who had access to the set.''

Crabtree nodded. ''But not anyone involved in the scene, so that lets out Diamond, Bill Connor, the camera crew, and all the technicians.'' He added to his list, speaking the name, ''Paul Diamond, leading actor.''

''Your security guards are supposed to stop unauthorized personnel from wandering around.''

''As soon as the sprinklers came on, a lot of people rushed around trying to find out how to turn them off, and Orliff checked with everybody. No one saw any strangers, so, yeah, it looks like someone on the set.''

''What about the way that this actor got sent to Niagara Falls? Who was it again, by the way?''

"Henry Vigor, the villain. Whoever did that had the call sheet for the day." He wrote Vigor's name on the place mat.

"Explain what that is." Salter began to feel that before he understood enough about moviemaking to investigate the case, this particular movie would be on late-night television.

"It's the sheet that's made up every night after the day's shooting to let everyone know who is on call the next day."

"So who would have had a copy?"

"I told you, it goes to everyone on call the next day."

"Can I get a list of everyone who had access to it that day?"

Crabtree looked bewildered. "I guess so. The call sheet itself tells you who had access to it. Everybody on the sheet. That's the point."

"Can I have a copy of it?"

"I'll tell Fay."

"Will that tell me everyone who is involved in the movie?"

"No, that's the crew list. I'll tell Fay to give you one of those, too." He glanced out the window. "There goes Josef, the director of photography. I have to get back to the office. I forgot he wanted to see me." He passed the place mat over to Salter.

"Couple more quick ones. Apart from personal spite, who would have an interest in wrecking the film? Would anyone stand to benefit?"

"I can't see how." Crabtree lifted himself off the seat, waiting for Salter's last question.

"I need an undercover man." Salter explained why he would like to have Ranovic and who would have to pay.

Crabtree sighed like the victim of a holdup who was trying to conceal his last twenty-dollar bill. "I guess so. Usual cop rates?"

Salter nodded. "He has to have a job, so maybe you could save someone's wages. What can you give him that won't attract attention. Could he be an extra?"

Crabtree shook his head. "Between the union and the casting agency he'd stick out like a sore thumb. I'd have a strike on my hands. Look, I've got to go. Call me this afternoon. I'll think of something." He paused. "I've had a thought. It wouldn't be a bad idea if word got around that you were there officially. What I mean is, they all know Orliff was retired, just an adviser. I'll say you're replacing him, but I'll drop a word in a couple of ears that you are really investigating the trouble. That way, the fact that you're there might make them quit."

"But if they don't, they just have to make sure I'm not around the next time they try something."

"Right, so we need someone they *don't* know about. Gotcha. What's his name?"

"Ranovic."

"Does he have another name?"

"I'll find out."

Crabtree made a note to himself on a pocket tape recorder.

"So if anyone wants to know, I'm still just the adviser."

"Yeah. Make sense?"

"I guess." Salter wanted to say something about the possibility that making thrillers had given Crabtree an instinct for this kind of thing, but he let it go. "When do you shoot next?"

"Sunday morning. St. Lawrence Market. The call is for five a.m."

They started to walk back to Crabtree's office. "Will I stick out on the set? Did Orliff watch every day?" Salter asked.

"You won't stick out. Besides, everybody's a groupie when a film's being made. If it weren't for the unions, I could get half the jobs done for nothing by people who want to hang around. Orliff was there all the time, too, until the bass season opened. Stay out of the way and no one will bother you." Crabtree shook Salter's hand to be rid of him and disappeared through the door of the fire station.

Salter followed him up the stairs and explained to the secretary about the copy of the call sheet and the crew list that Crabtree had promised him. He could have them right away, she said, and set about instructing her machine to produce copies.

Nothing that he had heard about so far seemed life threatening. When he got the lists from the secretary, he would have something to play with, though Crabtree had suggested that playing was all he would be doing. And then he had a lot of listening to do, familiarizing himself with the world he had found himself in.

THEIR SON, Seth arrived at the house on Saturday afternoon looking amused. He had visited his grandfather on the way home from rehearsal.

They left him alone until after supper; then Salter asked, as casually as he could, what his grandfather wanted him for.

"He just wanted to talk to me," Seth said.

It didn't sound as if Seth were standing on his six-teen-year-old "none-of-your-business-it's-my-private-life" dignity. More like a come-on.

"What about?" Salter risked.

"Sodomy."

"Ah." The most natural thing in the world. "What did he have to say about it?"

"He was against it."

Annie laughed a lot, and Seth went gleefully up-stairs. Salter realized he now had another adult on his hands who would soon be patting him tolerantly on the head.

FOUR

THE Saturday-morning-in-the-market scene was scheduled to be shot on Sunday, when the market was closed. When Salter arrived at six, it looked as if a hundred people had come together in response to a divine message, and they were now waiting for the holy presence to appear among them. Groups of people were sitting and standing around on the road between the two market buildings. A number of Winnebagos were lined up along Front Street; at the head of the line a giant trailer extruded power cables like intestines. But Salter could find no sign of a camera; there were no lights blazing; he heard no one shouting, "Cut," or, "Action."

He walked through the crowd, trying to overhear what was happening, taking the opportunity to mingle and listen to gossip. One group of women, dressed as Saturday morning shoppers, were comparing health clubs. Two or three youngish children were chasing each other in and out of the groups of adults. Outside the South Market a cellist was entertaining some other musicians—two with guitars, one with a tin whistle, and one with a harp, all actors impersonating the regular Saturday morning musicians. The cellist sounded to Salter extraordinarily good, and the contrast between the ramshackle look of his instrument and the music he was getting out of it seemed to enhance the beauty of the piece he was playing. Salter knew nothing about music, but he was perfectly capable of being infected by a piece when he was trapped by circumstances, usually in a car, in a receptive mood. He was once driving across the prairies, and at dusk on the second day he heard Dame Clara Butt singing "Abide With Me" on the car radio. He had thought that if he were a Manitoba farmer in the winter, in, say, 1903, wondering if he had salted enough pork to make it until spring, it might have been a comforting thing to hear.

This thing the cellist was playing would stay with him, he knew, and he waited for the musician to finish to congratulate him and ask him what it was. The cellist gave the instrument a spin and opened the back of the case, taking out a small tape. " 'Song without Words,'" he read off the tape. "Hang on, I'll play you the next one." He put the tape back into the recorder inside the case, pressed the "start" button, and picked up his bow, joining in after a few bars and bowing the silent strings with panache. Salter looked around at the grinning group of fake musicians.

"Geoff's our only real musician," the harpist said. "If you want to hear the rest of us, you'll have to wait for the sound track."

Salter moved on. In the center of all the inactivity he caught a glimpse of Crabtree, the producer, arguing passionately with what looked like an early Mennonite settler, a man with steel-rimmed glasses and a fringe of beard.

"I'm going to kill him," Crabtree was saying quietly but passionately. "I'm going to tie a herring across the top of his skull and drop him in the lake with floats under his arms, let the gulls get at him."

"Take it easy, Jack," the Mennonite said. "He's the only one of us that can handle Diamond, and Henry likes him, too."

"That's his way, d'ye see?" Crabtree said. "He's been kissing their asses from the start, and now he's indispensable. But I'm going to dispense with him. I think I'll impale him. I think that must be the worst, don't you, Bill? Could you direct a scene with impaling in it?" The words were spoken in a controlled conversational manner that in another man might be lighthearted, but Salter had the impression that this was the form Crabtree's anger took. He wasn't wasting his energy shouting. He was planning.

The Mennonite evidently thought so, too, because he continued to supply an urgent, soothing patter. Crabtree then caught sight of Salter. "You, Charlie," he called. "Where would I find someone who would break a couple of legs for me. For a price I'd pay whatever it costs."

"Now, now, Jack. We'll be rolling in a couple of minutes. You'll see." The Mennonite looked at Salter for help.

Not having the faintest idea of what was going on, Salter could only smile and give his head a little sideways flick to show he knew Crabtree was joking.

The producer seemed to calm down, and the Mennonite tried to look jovial, but he was sweating heavily, like a lion tamer who had mislaid his chair. "You taking over from Fred Orliff?" he asked. He put out his hand. "I'm Bill Connor, the director."

Just then the doors of the North Market opened, and two men came out. One of them was a bearded roughneck in his forties dressed in a dirty safari suit like an out-of-work big-game hunter. All his parts were moving rapidly as he danced around, pointing, shrugging, waving. The other man was absolutely still. He was in his late seventies.

The younger man looked up, saw the crowd, Salter's group among them, waved to the director, and spoke through a megaphone. "We're ready for you, Bill," his magnified voice boomed, and he turned back to the older man to continue what he was saying.

Crabtree, in his manic conversational voice, said to Connor, "He's ready for you, did you hear?" Then he made a dive forward, shouting in full volume, "I'll give you ready, you son of a bitch."

Instinctively, Salter jumped in front of Crabtree while Connor held on to him from behind.

"Jack," Connor pleaded. "He's here. Let's get the scene started."

It took a few minutes; then the producer sagged, and they sat him down on a low brick wall around a flower bed. The man in the safari suit watched them, apparently puzzled; beside him, the tall old man looked on without much interest.

Crabtree said, reverting to his conversational voice, "Promise me, Bill, that I can do what I like with him when this is over."

"It's a promise, Jack."

"Promise me this is the last time."

"This is the last time, Jack. I'll see to it."

"Then I can wait." The producer stood up and shouted, "All right. Let's get it set up. Tell Paul we're nearly ready."

Other voices took up the shout, and the crowd swirled into activity. From a trailer parked on Church Street, a small, dark, intense man in his early thirties

emerged holding a script. His self-absorption was like
a shield to move people out of his way as he moved to
walk through them, reading the script.

"Paul Diamond, this is Charlie Salter," Crabtree
said, but the actor walked past them on to Connor.
"You want me to react when I see him or afterward,
when I get to the other door?" he asked Connor.

"You should look him in the face as you pass him.
Then get to the other curb and look around. Then
back up to the door facing the street, then start coming forward, in shock, like, slowly at first, then at a
run."

The actor marked his script. "I'm carrying groceries, right?"

Connor nodded.

"What? What's in the bags?"

Connor looked around. A competent-looking girl
stepped forward. "Meat," she said. "You buy meat
in the South Market; then you go to the North Market for bread and flowers."

Diamond said, "There's a kosher butcher in the
South Market?"

The girl looked at him and shook her head slowly,
considering. "Make it oranges," she said. "There's a
guy sells oranges just inside the door."

Diamond marked his script. "You want me to drop
the bags when I go after him?"

"That's a long way off, Paul. See how we feel when
we get to that scene."

"There's nothing in the script."

"I know. We'll decide. You and me."

"Am I having a good time? What's the weather
like? What time is it? Do I come to the market all the
time?"

"Yes. You're a market freak. You come here every Saturday morning at seven. It's your turf. You expect to see people you've seen before. One or two. And it's a beautiful day. June."

"That's it. Okay. No more." Diamond walked away and hunched down against the wall with his script.

Now they were almost ready. Salter moved well away from the action to a spot where he could watch in comfort.

"Places everyone, please. I want absolute silence," Sherriff boomed through the megaphone.

"Roll tape," Connor, the director, shouted.

"Speed," someone else responded.

"Camera," Connor ordered.

"Rolling," the camera operator called.

"Action," Connor ordered.

A dozen extras crossed the street, six in each direction. Three more emerged from the door of the North Market, followed by the elderly actor. "Cut," Connor shouted. "How come Henry hasn't got his groceries? Where's props?"

The competent-looking girl stepped forward. "The stuff is here. He forgot to pick it up."

"That's not like Henry," a voice said. "He must be getting old at last."

The scene began again; this time the old man carried a plastic sack filled with groceries and a bunch of flowers.

"Cut," the director called. "No flowers. Let me see some chicken feet sticking out of the bag. This guy is European, German. They like to buy the whole bird."

It took an hour before Henry Vigor came through the door satisfactorily and the camera was repositioned for the next shot, the one of Diamond coming out of the South Market. Salter stayed watching on the perimeter of the action. At one point, he complimented three extras dressed as bums who were drinking sherry from a bottle. (On Saturday mornings the liquor store next to the market opens at seven, and some of Toronto's street people show their gratitude.) "When do you people get involved?" Salter asked one of the three, a middle-aged woman with matted hair wearing wrecked running shoes. "Fuck off," she said, showing the stumps of four teeth, and Salter realized that these three were real enough, left over from the day before.

When he had seen Diamond come through the door enough times, Salter found a table in the café and took out his copy of the script. As he sat down, a break was called, and the crowd drifted over to a catering truck that was dispensing coffee and croissants. Salter stayed where he was, and a girl came into the café and sat down at his table. She opened a large tapestry bag, releasing a powerful smell of camphor, took out a vacuum flask, and poured herself a cup of coffee, ignoring Salter.

Salter said, "Are you part of the scene?"

The girl looked straight ahead of her, like someone who does not wish to be involved with strangers. "I am the fourth A.D.," she said.

"What's that?"

Now the girl looked at him curiously and made a decision to talk to him. "There are four A.D.s, assistant directors. There's the first—he's the one that Mr. Crabtree wants to kill. Then there's the second: He is short, fat, and fair-haired, and he sweats a lot. He is looking after the actors going from one building to the other. Then there is the third A.D. He looks after the extras. That's him—see?—through the window, the pretty one. His father is one of the backers. He has a light meter around his neck in case the director of photography loses his."

"What do you do?"

"I run errands. I am a trainee. Everyone thinks I got the job by sleeping with the first A.D. and I am trying to learn everything I can about the business so that next time I can choose who people think I sleep with because I will have a proper job. My name is Helena Sukos." She said all this without attitude; she was simply describing the life of a fourth A.D. as she had experienced it.

She had a fan of frizzy hair partly obscuring one side of her face and a small mouth with badly cared-for teeth. Her accent was central European and English; she had picked up an Oxford drawl from her teacher, but she spoke with the pronounced sibilants and clear word endings of someone whose first language had more edges than English. These were the things Salter noticed. Her dress was made of some thin, dark, soft material, and she was wearing sandals. What Salter really noticed was that she was sexy, but he couldn't have said why. Salter guessed her age at about twenty-three or four.

He looked at her flask. "Don't you like the company coffee?"

"It's fine, but if I go out there, I'll be sent on an errand."

Salter pointed to the street. "Who is the pretty girl handing out groceries?"

She looked through the window. "Which one, the red-haired girl? She is working with props. The other one, the blonde, is the continuity girl, Carole Banjani."

"Like a fifth A.D.?"

"Oh, no. Her job is to make sure that the scenes match, that no one looks different in one part of a scene to the next. Also, she is continually keeping the script matching the film. If an actor changes a line, then she must type the line in the script right away. Two minutes later, he might ask her for his line, and he means the new one, the one they have just changed. No, that's a real job, and I would like to train for it. Most of all, though, I would like to learn about the camera. So I hang around everywhere, but mostly around the camera."

"Don't you have any real duties?"

"I told you, I run errands. I am a gofer. Is that right? Why don't you know this. What's your job?"

"I'm nobody, an outsider. I'm just advising on local stuff."

"You are a policeman."

"Is it that obvious?" Salter had tried to dress casually, even leaving off his tie.

"Not until you tell me you are advising. That's a policeman's answer. But why are there so many policemen around?"

"The ones in uniform are just off-duty, paid as security guards."

"No, no, I mean him, for instance." She pointed through the door.

Salter looked out, afraid he was going to see Constable Ranovic, but the girl was pointing to a young man who was leaning against a tree, away from the action. He looked like a physical education instructor. "He's not one of ours," he said.

"Of course he is. If you don't know him, then he's probably a secret service person."

"How can you tell?"

"Look at him! What else could he be?"

Looking at the man through the girl's obviously educated eyes, Salter saw that she was probably right. "Who's the guy next to him with the camera? He with the secret service, too?"

The girl laughed. "No, that's Terry Dresden. He's the stills man. He's taking pictures for publicity. He takes pictures of everything."

"Including the actual filming?"

"Oh, yes, to give to the newspapers for publicity. You know?"

Might be worth having a chat with, Salter thought. He turned back to Helena.

"Where did you get so much practice identifying cops?"

"In Bucharest, where I come from. With us it's second nature. Ah, here we go. Oh, no. They are talking again. Another half hour." She poured herself more coffee. "Would you like some of this?"

Salter shook his head.

On the sidewalk Bill Connor, the director, was arguing with Paul Diamond. The extras drifted back into little knots.

"What was Mr. Crabtree so mad about this morning?" Salter asked.

"He was angry because Tom Sherriff, the first A.D., had not done his job again. He is supposed to have everything ready, but he overslept, I think. I wasn't with him last night." She looked at Salter over her coffee. "He's done it before, and whenever he does it, it costs thousands of dollars."

"He was here. He was inside with that old actor."

"No, no. He's a great bullshit man. He got here an hour late. He picked up Henry—that's the old actor—at his hotel and brought him to the back door so he could come out the front talking to Henry as if he had been inside for hours."

"Why don't they get rid of him?" Salter already knew the answer to this, but he wanted to keep Helena talking.

"Because Henry Vigor, the old actor, as you call him, and Paul Diamond, the other star, want him. He has made himself their friend, and now they go to him for everything, especially Henry, who doesn't like to be left alone. So poor Jack has to put up with him. Look, now, at Henry."

Across the street, the elderly actor was asking something of the people around him, looking distressed, and Sherriff appeared from the crowd and took his arm and led him back into the building. Sherriff reappeared and called for someone through his megaphone. The call got taken up until it reached Salter. Salter said, "They're asking for someone called Helena."

"Oh, God, that's me." The girl gathered up her flask and slipped it into her odorous bag. "They want me to sit with Henry." She ran through the door and across the street, the huge bag banging against her hip.

Salter followed her out and crossed to the North Market to watch the scene begin. The chanted litany of commands and responses leading to "Action" began, and the extras swirled purposefully back and forth from building to building until Diamond emerged from the South Market, looking, Salter had to admit, both like the star and exactly like a man enjoying his Saturday morning shopping. The two actors crossed in mid-street, bumped, and Diamond gave Vigor a nod due a faintly familiar face. The camera was set up to catch Diamond nod, continue on his way, then look reflective, then, alarmed, turn and start back across the street. They did it four times; then the camera was repositioned to take the same scene, this time focusing on Vigor. After they had shot this several times, it was lunchtime.

Salter, remembering the scenes he had heard discussed, figured it would take all afternoon to film Diamond searching the South Market for Vigor, and he went to look for something to eat. He followed the crew into the North Market, which had been set up as a restaurant and now looked like the monthly dinner meeting of the Lions' Club. Not sure he would be able to choose his seat and not wanting to answer too many questions about himself yet, Salter turned back into Front Street and found a small truck dispensing fruit juice, coffee, and doughnuts to those who preferred not to eat the lunch provided. He joined the small lineup, picked up a cruller and coffee, and found a place to sit down outside the market.

FIVE

GRADUALLY DURING the afternoon, he began to get some idea of the order inside the chaos. There was no real need for him to stay, but he was far too interested on this first day to leave until the shooting was over. It was a beautiful day, and there was nothing to rush home for.

Early in the afternoon he located the makeup truck and its driver, Constable Ranovic, who was chatting with the drivers of the other trucks. Crabtree had found a good cover for the policeman. Once the makeup truck was parked, there was nothing for the driver to do until the day was over, giving Ranovic plenty of time and opportunity to wander around, listening.

Crabtree had got Ranovic in place by simply asking the drivers' captain if he could supply a union card for an undercover cop. He told him exactly why they needed an undercover man and pointed out that if Ranovic could pose as a member of the drivers' union, then Walsh, the drivers' captain, would be the only one who knew who he was. On the other hand, if they had to find another cover, then the captain would be wondering all the time which one was the cop.

The drivers' captain recognized his duty and came up with the notion of giving Ranovic a temporary card as a member of an affiliate union from Alberta and assigning him to the makeup truck whose driver had just quit. At the time, none of the other drivers had buddies or brothers-in-law who were waiting to get jobs on the set, so it worked. Salter wondered what else had passed between Crabtree and Walsh, feeling instinctively that *something* extra had been required.

As Salter passed the group of drivers who were arguing about baseball, he heard Ranovic ask who he, Salter, was. When he looked back, they were all looking at him without much curiosity, and he turned back to them to see what Ranovic was playing at. "Any idea what time they'll be finished?" he asked the group.

"When it gets dark," the nearest man said. "You the retired cop?"

"That's right."

"Keep it that way, eh?" Ranovic said, jocular, impudent, acting like mad. Some of the other drivers grinned. One of them pulled down his cap to cover his face, a clownish effort not to be recognized.

Salter went on his way, wondering if show business might not go to Ranovic's head.

THE SCENE IN the South Market called for Paul Diamond to move around quickly, looking for Vigor, while Vigor, unaware of Diamond following him, stayed just out of reach.

As the first shot of the rear view of Vigor began, a woman's voice cut through the action. "Stop it, Bill. He's got the wrong bag." It was Carole Banjani, the continuity girl, who had moved in front of the camera.

"What are you talking about?" Crabtree wanted to know. He was standing on the edge of the scene.

Carole Banjani ignored him and walked over to Bill Connor, the director. "Here. Here's the picture." She held up a Polaroid shot. "He should be carrying a bag with chicken feet sticking out of it."

"Are you sure?" Crabtree, who had moved in toward them, asked.

Banjani pushed a strand of hair under a loose bun on her neck. She was a good-looking woman in her late thirties who gave the impression she had slept in her clothes and her makeup. Everything was tidied into place, but the line of her lips was smudged, and the mascara on one eye was slightly smeared. To Salter she looked as if she had avoided washing that morning. The impression was strengthened by the slightly tawdry formality of black tights and a dusty-looking pair of pumps, which made her legs stand out in the sea of blue jeans and running shoes. After poking back her hair, she picked up her clipboard and addressed Crabtree directly. "I'm getting a little confused," she said. "My job is to look after continuity. For Bill. Right?"

"Why is Henry having so much trouble getting the bag straight?" Crabtree asked.

"That's something between you and Mr. Vigor. My job is to make sure that the scenes match."

Crabtree shrugged and walked away. Banjani smiled at Connor and showed him the Polaroid again.

"I'm sorry," Vigor said, holding up the right shopping bag and pointing to the chicken's feet. "I picked the other one up at the door. My mistake."

Her point made, Banjani made a show of checking the rest of Vigor against the picture, then nodded to Connor that she was satisfied.

As the scene was being shot for the second or third time, the writer, Stanley Fisher, burst, screaming, into the action.

WHEN FISHER HAD BEEN escorted outside, Salter, back watching from the tactful distance of the coffee counter in the southwest corner of the market, felt a hand rest familiarly on his arm. He looked up to a thin, smiling, gentle face, inches from his own, belonging to a man in his mid to late fifties, very thin, and well over six feet tall. The voice was accented. European of some kind, not French or Italian. Salter tried to put some space between them, but the hand was firm. "Josef Hodek, director of photography. What advice do you have for us today, Mr. Policeman?"

He had seen Hodek around all day and guessed he was something to do with the technical side. Salter wriggled slightly, a hooked fish. "It's not a police problem," he said. This was show business, and the man was a foreigner. Go with the flow. Europeans had different body language. It didn't mean anything.

The hand left his arm, then reappeared on his shoulder. "Let's have a cup of coffee. They will be a long time on this."

In front of the cheese stall a script conference was taking place. Did they need the scene that Diamond had eliminated?

Diamond said, "Not in the middle of the chase."

"Right, Paul. Right. It should come after, when you've lost Henry. Let's do it now, while we're set up here. Okay, Mac?" he asked the actor in the cheese stall.

"George," the actor said. "George Makepeace," adding, quietly but clearly, "*Do* try to remember." Then, booming, "Ready when you are, chief."

They began to set up for the scene, and Salter allowed himself to be led to a seat by the director of photography, who collected some coffee from the actor who was manning the coffee stall and sat down across from Salter at the one little table provided. He made a gesture of salutation with his cup.

"Who told you who I was?" Salter asked, wondering what this instant friendship was all about.

"My friend, Mr. Orliff."

Salter swallowed some coffee, trying to picture Orliff arm in arm with the director of photography.

Hodek nodded himself along. "He told me he was leaving and someone else would be advising, and who else could you be? Actually, Helena just told me."

"The assistant-director girl?"

Hodek nodded. "She is a friend of mine. So what do you think of our film so far?"

"It's an eye-opener."

Hodek erupted with glee and looked around to see if he could find someone to share Salter's remark with. "An eye-opener," he spluttered. "Yes. An eye-opener. You should have my job. That is what I have to create. An eye-opener. Wonderful." He looked at Salter admiringly.

"You turn the camera?"

Hodek roared again with laughter, making a motion of someone turning a crank. "Like this?" Then he turned serious. "No, no. I am director of photography. I explain to the cameraman, and the cameraman goes like this." Once more Hodek made his cranking motion. He patted Salter's hand. "As you are in charge of the police."

"I'm not in charge of anything, Josef. I'm just the adviser. Off-duty, that's me."

"Sure, sure, sure, sure," Hodek said, patting away. "And what about the secret service man? Is he helping you to advise?"

"I'm telling you, I'm not working here. I'm just an expert. That's it, I'm an expert, not a cop today." As he spoke, he wondered if he should whisper a word in the secret service man's ear about how public he had become. He decided that could wait until he found out what the guy was doing, which he planned to do the next day. He also wondered what Hodek's interest in him was. As far as he could tell, Hodek's intimacy was purely central European.

"I bet you do not even have a gun on you," Hodek said.

"Of course not. I don't carry one unless I have to, and sometimes not even then."

"Mr. Orliff was the same. A beautiful man."

Salter, once more thinking of the man who had never said a personal word during their entire relationship, was confounded.

"I am going to visit him at his cottage in the country," Hodek said. "Have you been there?"

"No, I haven't."

"You are not friends? He likes you very much."

"Does he? Yeah, well, I like him." We've never actually kissed, though, Salter thought. "Tell me what was going on over there. What was the problem?"

Hodek waved his hand. "The same as always. Fisher does not like to see his words changed. Diamond thinks he knows better and wishes to look good. Bill Connor, too."

"And Jack? Jack Crabtree?"

"Mr. Crabtree must try to make a profit or he will not produce any more films. He must not let this one get upset. They are all very nice people, but they have different ideas." Suddenly, Hodek became confidential, beckoning Salter another inch closer. "Let me see if I can explain. Some are more important than others. Paul and Henry, the two leading actors, are very important. Paul is a local boy makes good. Canadian, but doing well in Hollywood. Henry is English, and he is very well known for playing German villains. Bill Connor, the director, is very talented, but he is from Newfoundland, and this is his first feature film, so Paul and Stanley Fisher do not respect him."

"And Fisher?"

"Stanley thinks that none of these people can be trusted with his picture. For him this is second best, and he wants to watch everything to see they are doing it right. Even me."

"And what was going on with Vigor's bag of groceries?"

Now Hodek looked anxious and lowered his voice. "Jack should not be interfering," he said. "Carole is a lovely girl, very good at her job, and the producer must not interfere with her."

"She was telling him to butt out? Crabtree? The boss?"

"Yes. She has a job to do. She would tell Eisenstein to butt out."

Salter looked incredulous.

"Otherwise, there would be chaos," Hodek said. "Carole is not tactful at the moment with Jack, but she is very nice."

Salter realized he was going to have to make his own adjustments to Hodek's character studies. For Hodek, everyone was nice, even the people he didn't like.

He wanted no enemies, and perhaps this desire lay behind his present approach to Salter.

"What about you, Josef?" he asked. "Are you important?"

"They could replace me, but I am not in anyone's way. I just look after the light. Without me it would be black. That's all a film is, you know, a few chemicals which have been struck by light. Another way to describe me is to say I make nice pictures of whatever they tell me to. I am cheap and I am good. In Czechoslovakia I was one of the best, but you have to make adjustments when you change countries. At least I am not a writer. Sometimes a writer cannot adjust."

"When did you leave Czechoslovakia?"

"In 1968, of course. I emigrated when the Russians came back."

Emigrated. What did that mean? "Really emigrated?",

"I got a visa to visit West Germany just before the tanks arrived. Everyone said they would not dare. Have you seen a picture called *The Unbearable Lightness of Being*? I was a pessimist. I left with my wife just in time. I came to this beautiful country, and I have been here very happily ever since."

"You like it here?"

Hodek threw his arms in the air and shook his head six or seven times to show he was amazed. "Everyone in Canada always asks that. One day I will say, 'No, I have applied for a visa to move to Liberia.' Of course I like it here. This is my home. I want to build a cottage, like Mr. Orliff. Besides, I have almost no friends left in Prague."

"You never hear from there?"

Hodek shrugged and waggled his hand back and forth. "Sometimes."

"Things have changed. Won't you go back there now? To live and work?"

Hodek took a breath. "I want to be sure how much they have changed. Oh, of course, it is wonderful, but they have a lot of things to work out, and I could be sitting on my thumbs for a long time while they are debating. They will not be making many films yet, and when they do, there are several photographers who have been in jail and will thus have more right to the work than me. Priorities of suffering will be established, and I will not rank so high." It was clear that Hodek had worked this out sometime before; he was answering a routine question now.

"What about the girl I was talking to, Helena? Does she live here now?"

"Helena is not Czech."

Salter was slightly embarrassed. "No, I know, she's from Romania, but I thought maybe you and her..." His voice trailed off.

"No. I helped her to get the job, but that was mainly Tom Sherriff. You think everybody in central Europe knows each other? We are all Ruritanians together? I've never been to Romania. Helena and I are friends, and we both dislike the Communists, but that is all. She was an interpreter in Bucharest, and they trusted her two years ago to go with some tourists across the border and she never went back." Hodek's politeness did not diminish, but Salter's ignorance seemed to have put a slight damper on their conversation.

"I'd like to see Czechoslovakia," Salter offered. It was something to say.

"I would like to show it to you, but I have no plans to go back yet."

A call traveled across the crowd. It was Sherriff's megaphone. Faces turned toward them. "They want me," Hodek said, and patted Salter's arm and left.

OUTSIDE THEY WERE setting up for the shot of Diamond running out of the market and looking for Vigor. Salter walked over to the commissary truck and begged yet another coffee. Fisher was sitting by the truck in a canvas chair, watched at a distance by a security guard. He was slumped, sullen, looking to Salter as if he needed company, but everyone was keeping clear. Salter leaned against the truck a few feet from him. The writer turned and stared at Salter.

"Charlie Salter. Remember? I'm the adviser on police stuff. I'm sorry I had to grab you in there. An old habit when you see guys fighting."

Fisher shrugged. "They could use some advice around here. You know anything about making movies?"

Salter shook his head.

Helena appeared with a clipboard in hand. "They want to know if there is usually a policeman controlling pedestrians across the street between the markets."

"No," Salter said. "Not at seven o'clock."

"Tell them to read the goddamn script," Fisher said. "If there were a cop there, I would have put one in. I've done my homework."

"I'll tell them." As she left, she said to Salter, "You were talking to Josef."

"He was telling me how much he liked my old boss, Mr. Orliff."

She smiled and left on her errand.

"Josef's okay," Fisher said, apparently contrasting the photographer with everyone else on the set.

"He's a very friendly guy."

"We're good friends. I understand where he comes from. I was in Czechoslovakia."

"When?"

"Two years ago, for ten days. I got to understand the Czechs."

"You speak Czech?"

"Some. I pick up languages fast. They were terrific people. Really took me into their homes. I made a lot of good friends."

"You were on holiday there?"

"I was invited. My books are translated there, and through most of Europe."

Fisher was not so much talking to Salter as letting Salter talk to him. He addressed all his remarks to the air around him, as if Salter were a promising reporter filling up the time for him until a nationally known, prettier, or otherwise more worthwhile interviewer with a better time slot showed up.

Salter felt himself on delicate ground. He had never heard of Fisher before, let alone read one of his books. He said, "I guess in those days it would have been hard to move around easily. Were there any regular tourists?"

"Sure, but they all had official guides who showed them what the government wanted them to see and told them the party line. I got past all that."

"How?"

Fisher grinned. "Pilsner," he said. "I went on a pub crawl with my interpreter. He was no different from any other guide at first, but after three or four beer halls I guess he was dying to break down. We found ourselves in a joint that was as noisy as one of those old beer parlors on Queen Street—do they still have them here?—and I guess he felt pretty safe, so he really gave it to me. Jiri Hof his name was. At the time, we were just hearing about *glasnost* and *perestroika* in Moscow, and I knew more about what was happening than he did. He told me it would never change in Czechoslovakia, that too many people had too much to lose. Then he let it all hang out, how much he hated the system. I got a real story out of it. The Communists still made good beer."

Fisher seemed to have ended his reminiscences. His memories were not turning into anecdotes but remaining as fragments. Salter changed the subject to introduce his real interest. "Got a little hot and heavy for a while in there," he said.

"Diamond thinks he's Al Pacino and Dustin Hoffman all rolled into one. He thinks he's a writer, too. Fact is, he's a third-rate actor who's done two movies of the week. Up here that makes him big. He's a prick and an asshole, and one day he'll get what's coming to him. And that goddamn director. What the fuck does he know? He's never even made a picture except some National Film Board documentary about growing up on the prairies. He knows about that, all right."

"Newfoundland."

"What?" For Fisher, every word spoken to him was a challenge, a provocation.

"Connor is from Newfoundland. He wouldn't know about the prairies."

Fisher gave a violent shrug of indifference. The conversation had gone as far as it could go. Salter put his cup back, nodded to Fisher, and moved off. Ten yards away he glanced back. The writer was slumped in his chair, staring at the backs of people watching the scene being shot. Everybody was making a wide detour around him.

HENRY VIGOR WAS the only actor Salter recognized. He had played dozens of villains, usually German, but to an Anglo-Saxon ear he could stand in for most of the central and Eastern European nationalities. When his part of the scene was finished, he immediately started calling for Sherriff. The assistant director appeared out of the crowd.

"I want to go home," Vigor said.

"Can you hang on a few minutes, Henry? I'll drive you myself then. I could send you now in the limousine, if you want. Whichever. But I'd rather take you myself. A lot of tourists around on Sundays. You'd be mobbed at the hotel."

"All right, I'll wait. Where shall I sit?"

Sherriff snapped his fingers, and the third assistant director appeared with two canvas chairs, one of which he opened for Vigor. Sherriff bustled about, looking for a way to keep Vigor amused, noticed Salter, introduced himself, took Salter to Vigor, introduced him, placing the other chair for him. Now Vigor had someone to talk to and look after him.

Salter saw that Vigor was older than he seemed, perhaps eighty. Acting, he looked fifteen years younger, but now, at the end of the day, he needed a minder.

"There's a lot of waiting around in your job," Salter said. A chat with Vigor, if he could manage it, was something to take home to Annie. ("Henry was telling me today..." "Henry?" "Henry Vigor. We were chatting during a break...")

"And in yours," Vigor said.

This was polite of him. "Can I get you anything?" Salter asked.

"Ask Tom where my bag is, would you?"

Salter caught the eye of the third assistant director and relayed the message. Sherriff appeared with a small leather bag from which Vigor produced a flask and poured out a cup of something brown and hot. He drank most of it in a gulp and refilled the plastic cup.

Salter said, "How long before you're finished?"

"They say six shooting days. Then I can go home." He turned slightly to face Salter. "You are Canadian, Mr. Salter? A real Canadian?" He was perking up slightly.

"The Indians claim that they are the only real Canadians. The rest of us are immigrants. But I was born here. So was my father. Why?"

"Nobody else seems to be. Tell me, what shall I buy for my daughter who is fifteen? What can I take back for her? Something Canadian."

Butter tarts? Maple syrup? That cheese made by Quebec monks, Oka? A video of *Anne of Green Gables*? *Fifteen*! Salter looked at Vigor with new respect. "Americans buy English bone china," he said.

"That I have. She is keen on horses. Can you think of anything Canadian to do with horses. Do the Indians make saddles?"

"My guess is that anything that she could use we get from England."

"Then perhaps water. We live on the Thames, and she is a bit of a water rat."

"You could take her back a canoe," Salter said. "We make those ourselves. Be hard to get on the plane, though," he added to show he was being flippant.

Vigor looked at him in wonder. "You are a genius. A canoe. Of course. Don't worry about the plane. I never fly. I am going home by sea on the *Q.E.2.* I can take a canoe. What a wonderful idea."

They were interrupted by Tom Sherriff, who was now ready to take Vigor home. "Ah, Tom, Mr. Salter has made a wonderful suggestion. You remember we were trying to think of something to take home to Camilla. Mr. Salter has suggested a canoe. Would you find out please where I can get one, and we will go and buy it."

"A canoe? You mean a toy, like?" Sherriff looked at Salter as he spoke.

"No, no. A real canoe she can use on the river."

"A collapsible one? I'll find out and have it sent."

"No, a proper one. I'd like to see it first."

"A canoe. A real one. Okay, I'll find out where. Now we need to get you home."

As Vigor was packing away his flask and getting himself upright, Sherriff said to Salter, "You get any more ideas, let me know first, okay? You're a real prince, you know that?"

In the yard, after supper that night, Salter said, "Henry was asking me today where he could find a canoe."

"Henry?" Annie leaned over to flick an ant off the table. "Henry who?"

"Henry Vigor, the actor. We saw him the other night on television. He played the guy who tried to get away dressed as a woman in that spy movie."

Seth looked up sharply. *"He's* in your movie! Boy. Can I come and watch?"

Salter wished for a moment that he had not succumbed to name-dropping. "Nobody's allowed on the set without authorization," he said. "What's the matter with your glasses?"

Seth removed his glasses, which were wire rimmed, with electrical tape apparently holding the bridge together. He looked at them severely, shrugged, and put them back on. In fact, the bridge was quite whole, but when Seth had recently been discovered to be in need of glasses for the first time, he had typically found his own way of enjoying them. Seth had just emerged from his earnest or ecological period and now was going through a phase that required that his clothes and other accoutrements allow him to inhabit an imaginary world more entertaining than the real one. The broken glasses and an old dirty raincoat he had found in a church bazaar turned him (in his own eyes) into the image of a brilliant émigré, probably a poet. He rode to school on a huge English lady's sit-up-and-beg bicycle that said to him that he had recently been riding down a leafy Surrey lane in 1921 and had taken a wrong turn into Toronto in 1991. Anything to relieve the tedium of being Seth.

"Don't change the subject," he said. "Why can't I watch?"

Annie said, "Take him with you. He'll stay out of the way. Won't you, Seth?"

"I'll have to check with the producer."

"Just take him. Who is going to object? Are they filming tomorrow?"

"Tomorrow's no good. They're starting at five a.m. I'll have to be up at four."

"I'll get up, Dad." Now Seth looked about thirteen, begging to be taken to a ball game.

"Don't you have rehearsal?"

"Not till nine. Where's it at?"

"The St. Lawrence Market."

"That's right by where we have to rehearse. I could come down and go straight on to rehearsal."

"All right, all right. I'll take you down, but if anyone objects, don't kick up a fuss, okay? Just go."

"Papa, I'll be a fly on the wall," Seth said in the voice of a consumptive child of five. "Can I bring Sam?"

"Sam who?"

"My buddy."

"No, for Chrissake. What do you think this is? If you're ready at four o'clock, I'll take you. I won't even wake you up."

"I'll wake you up, Seth," Annie said. "He always wakes *me* up on Sunday mornings."

"Tomorrow's Monday," Salter said. "*This* was Sunday. Remember?"

"Right," said Annie. "So it was."

Salter said, "You'd better go to bed if you're going to be alive at four o'clock."

Seth saluted and marched off.

"Who else did you meet on the set?" Annie asked when they were alone.

Salter described the people in his day, eventually coming to Helena Sukos. "Kind of a European counterculture type," he said. "You know, a dress made of some thin, dark stuff, clinging but shapeless, doesn't comb her hair, and needs a dentist badly. But still sexy."

"In what way?"

Salter thought about it. "She reminds me of a description of French girls I read somewhere. The reason they look and walk sexy is that they spend all their money on pretty underwear so they *feel* sexy and it shows."

"And this—Helena—had nice underwear, did she?"

Salter, after a good dinner, caught up in his fancy, missed the signals entirely. "Yeah," he said, "I would think so."

SIX

THE SCENES SCHEDULED for Monday morning involved Henry Vigor walking along Front Street and getting into his car. In the time scale of the script, the scenes took place a week later, when Diamond had staked out the market on the following Saturday morning and sighted Vigor as he was leaving, then followed him to his home in Oakville. Most of the action involved Diamond sitting in his car, watching the crowds, and Connor decided to shoot these scenes first.

Salter found Crabtree giving instructions to Carole Banjani, the continuity girl, and cleared with him that Seth could watch, then took the boy over to the Winnebago, where Vigor was already sitting, drinking the brown liquid from his flask.

"Mr. Salter," Vigor greeted him, looking considerably stronger and flatteringly pleased to see him. "Who is this?"

Salter introduced Seth, who was shining with happiness, his role-playing forgotten.

"Tom!" Vigor called. "Bring us some more chairs. Sit down, Seth. Tell me, do you know anything about canoes?"

Seth looked shyly at his father, who shrugged, indicating that it was up to Seth to get on with it. "Sure," Seth said. "I was a camp counselor last summer. Well, sort of."

"What's that? Sit down, my boy. Charlie, get Seth a cup of cocoa or something."

Seth smiled at seeing his father made an errand boy and explained to Vigor what a camp counselor did.

"That's wonderful!" Vigor exclaimed. "Would you come with us and choose a canoe for my daughter? I don't think Tom knows very much about them. He was never a camp counselor, I think. Now, tell me about what happens next. Are you going to be a policeman, like your father?"

"A *cop*!" Seth was jerked out of his diffidence by the idea. "No way! I'm going to be a dancer."

Vigor took a sip of his beef tea, or soup, or kvass. "Ballet?"

"I hope so."

"It's a hard life."

That's the spirit, thought Salter.

"That's what I want to do, though."

Vigor looked at Seth as if he were appraising a horse and changed the subject. "So will you help me to buy a canoe?"

"Sure. Yeah, sure."

"Good. Tell me about your school. How old are you? Do you study Shakespeare in Canada? Of course you do. What Shakespeare did you study last year?"

Seth told him about *A Midsummer Night's Dream*.

"Do you know any by heart?"

"Not from that. I didn't have any lines. I know the Duke's speech from *As You Like It*, though. I had to write it out twenty-five times."

"But I *am* the Duke! Recite it to me. Let's see if we both remember."

Salter left them there and wandered over to watch the filming of Diamond in his car. When the scene was

over, the call came for Vigor to get ready to do his
scene. He was still talking to Seth. As Salter approached, he heard Vigor say, "I know. Iambic pen-
tameter has five feet, but the line nearly always has
four stresses when you speak it. Try it again. Like this:
Now my *co-mates* and *brothers* in exile. Two stresses
for 'co-mates,' I think, and one each for 'now' and
'brothers.' *Hath* not old *cust*om made this life *more
sweet* . . . etc."

"NOW my CO-MATES and BROTHERS in EXILE," Seth
spat out.

"No, no," Vigor said. "Like this."

They were interrupted by Sherriff, who took Vigor
away to work.

"You haven't seen any of the filming yet," Salter
said to Seth. "I didn't want to break in after Mr. Vigor
started to talk to you."

"That's okay. I'll watch this bit. Jesus, Dad. He's
terrific," and he turned and punched Salter hard in the
stomach to express his happiness.

Salter doubled over, only half-pretending, and
straightened up to two faces: Seth's, dismayed and
concerned—"Dad, you okay?"—and Helena Sukos;
looking at both of them as if she had just glimpsed a
side of the human animal more savage than she had
ever been aware of.

"My son Seth," Salter gasped as quickly as he
could, making the introduction to cover his distress,
or rather, his embarrassment at that distress. "Helena Sukos. Works on the film."

"Do you often punch your father in the belly?"
Helena asked Seth.

"I *used* to. I won't anymore. You okay, Dad?"

"Yeah, yeah, yeah. What's going on, Helena?"

"Henry is getting ready to walk along the street for the fourth time. They don't need me for the moment. What are you doing here, Seth?"

"What do you do, miss?" Seth asked at the same moment.

"I am the fourth assistant director."

Salter waited for her to add the information that her job was to sleep with the first assistant director and run errands, but Helena continued. "The errand person. Nobody, really. Have you ever watched a film being made?"

Seth shook his head, young enough to see her as the most interesting schoolteacher he had ever met, old enough to imagine her outside the classroom.

"Come on, then. I'll explain what they are doing." She held out her hand, and Seth, interpreting the sign correctly, moved toward her as her arm came around him in a mothering gesture. Salter watched them move off, feeling the soreness in his stomach, wondering if Seth wasn't getting beyond needing a big sister.

AN HOUR LATER, the Monday morning workers were arriving in Market Square, making it difficult to continue, and Connor decided he had enough to be able to put the scene together. All the plugs were pulled, and Seth emerged from the crowds alone.

"Where's Helena?" Salter asked.

"Some guy hollered for her. She's nice, isn't she, Dad? How did you get to know her?"

"The same way you did. I was looking for someone to show me around. Time you were gone."

"Don't fuss, Pop. I've got a watch. I've got time to *hop* to my class."

Salter left him there and made his own way over to the line of Winnebagos where Ranovic was waiting for the makeup people to pack up. "You guys finished for the day?" Salter asked him.

"As soon as these people are gone. How about you?"

"I've got work to do. I'll be in my office for the rest of the day."

"Good luck," Ranovic said. "See you tomorrow, I guess. Hey, Fred," he called to another driver. "Where are we tomorrow?"

Salter found his car and drove back to College Street; two hours later, Ranovic joined him.

"SO WHAT do you think?" Salter asked. Picking up gossip, comparing impressions, was all they could do at this stage.

Ranovic hitched his chair forward. "The old guy, Vigor, he's terrific. You notice the way he turns on when they shout, 'Action!'? I was watching him to-day. It's like he switches a light on inside. Then, when they stop, he switches off, without moving. It's in-credible. Paul Diamond is okay, too. He's got some nice moves. Reminds me of Richard Dreyfuss. Re-member him in *The Tin Men*? Some of the extras, though, they'll never make it. I'd kinda like to try that myself. Do you think the producer would let me? Be one of the crowd?"

"That's wonderful. I'll pass all this on to Crabtree. Now you've told me what Central Casting thinks, could I hear from Officer Ranovic? Got anything for me?"

"Sorry, chief. I was just—you know. It's interest-ing as hell, isn't it?" Ranovic smiled, unapologetically, then pulled out his notebook. "Here's what I've got so far. One: It could be union trouble. That's what the truck drivers think. It's the only kind of trouble they know. Not their union, of course. ACTRA. See, Diamond and Vigor are imports, and they don't like that. ACTRA, I mean. But I asked a couple of extras, and they just laughed. Diamond is Canadian; he's still a member of ACTRA. Besides, ACTRA isn't the IATZE."

Salter looked at him, waiting.

"IATZE," repeated Ranovic. "The drivers. Me."

Salter nodded, waiting.

"One guy suggested maybe the teamsters. See, they wanted to take over from the IATZE a while ago. They made a few moves. Coincidentally, some tires got slashed, but we hung in there."

"So scrub ACTRA and the Teamsters. Who else?"

"Could be a loose cannon."

"For Christ's sake, talk English."

"I mean, someone's gone berserk. Guy who hates films. Getting some kind of revenge."

Salter looked at Ranovic in a way that made the constable shift back in his chair and shrug his shoulders.

"What have you seen or heard? Never mind the speculation. I'll do that."

"Diamond doesn't like Vigor. Vigor doesn't like Diamond. The writer, Fisher, doesn't like anybody. Nobody likes the writer. Crabtree will kill Sherriff, that assistant director, as soon as the movie's finished, and, oh, yes, the continuity girl, Carole, is on the outs with Crabtree."

"Finally something I didn't know. What does 'on the outs' mean?"

"They've had a fight. They're lovers. Didn't you know?"

"No, she didn't tell me. You sure?"

"Everybody knows. Well, everybody in the makeup truck. Those two makeup guys spend all their time talking about who's diddling who. It's like the locker room of a girls' basketball team. All I have to do is say a name and away they go, I get the whole rundown. So the story on Crabtree is that he and Carole are on the outs. Crabtree likes to spread himself around, and Carole thinks he's been making it with one of the kids."

"Has he?"

"Probably. Derek—that's the head makeup man—he says Crabtree has always had it on for young girls. Carole Banjani used to be one of his young girls, so she knows where he's at, and she's pushing forty right now, so she wants to nail him down. So Derek says. But right now she thinks he's got something going with some new kid."

"I'd have thought he had too much on his mind. But is Banjani up to wrecking the movie to get back at him? Wait a minute." Salter looked at a list on his desk. "She's on the edge of every scene. The way I understand it, she couldn't have turned on the sprinkler if she was doing her job."

Ranovic spread his arms in a gesture that accepted that Salter knew what he was talking about. "That's all I've heard so far. But they're only just starting to include me in the talk. If you want to know anything about anybody, tell me his name, and I'll feed it to Derek. He and Neville know everything. Neville's the other makeup guy."

"We haven't got a hell of a lot to go on. There's no point in trying to figure out who made the phone calls. I'll have a look at the studio where the sprinklers came on, but from what I've seen, all we can do is eliminate a handful of people. By the time they realized what was happening, there were dozens of people running around trying to switch off the water. Any one of them could have switched it on." The smell of Ranovic's deodorant wafted powerfully across Salter's desk. "Your cover still good?" Salter asked.

"Of course!" It was like asking Henry Vigor if he could do a Hungarian accent.

"Then you should stay with it, I guess."

Ranovic stood up and moved behind his chair. "Do you have an extra copy of the script?" he asked.

"No. What do you want it for? There aren't any parts left."

Ranovic smiled and looked sheepish. "I ought to know what's happening, don't you think?"

"Can't you find one around the makeup crew? Or one of the truck drivers?"

"Those guys don't even *watch*. I figured—"

Salter slid his own copy across the desk. "Photocopy it. Bring mine back before you go. And leave yours at home. For all I know, it's illegal to copy the script."

Ranovic left, reading.

SALTER WALKED DOWNSTAIRS a flight to the intelligence unit. Sergeant Parker, in charge of the group, had talked to Orliff and had promised to inform him if any of the known right wing activists had surfaced near the film.

Above the rank of constable, policemen behind desks are of two kinds. Either they look temporary, caught in flight, as if they are borrowing the desk to make out a report. They keep their jackets on and write square to the desk like someone taking an examination. Their raincoats are ready, often lying across the back of another chair. The other kind look home at last, in shirtsleeves usually; a large, untidy pile of permanent-looking paperwork covers the desk; a coffeepot bubbles; a jacket is hidden away in a cupboard. Parker was of the second kind. His office was his nest, a burrow he had hollowed out that he hated to leave. He did not ever expect to be asked to take part in an outdoor operation again.

"We don't have a thing for you," he said. "None of the people we know are involved. But there's a guy you ought to meet in from Ottawa. He'll be back in a few minutes. From the CSIS. Ever occur to you, Charlie, that only in Canada does the secret service call itself the secret service, even on their calling cards? There has to be a reason."

"Looks like a high school football coach? Fair hair, blue blazer?"

"That's him. You know him?"

"I've seen him flitting about. What's he up to?"

"He'll tell you. Making sure this thing's got no ramifications for the spooks."

"I think it's personal."

"That's what Orliff thought. Here's the guy now. Constable Gudgeon. This is Staff Inspector Salter, who's investigating the trouble on the film set."

"Good to meet you, Staff. How's it going?" Gudgeon sat down and placed a neatly brogued foot on the other knee. He picked up a paperweight from the Intelligence officer's desk and turned it over in his hand, then looked from under his eyebrows at Salter.

They're all bloody actors, Salter thought. This guy's playing "The Man from Headquarters." How old was he? Twenty-three? "It isn't," Salter said. "How about you?"

Gudgeon made a wiggling noncommittal gesture with his head. He fingered the paperweight as if looking for a secret compartment.

Salter said, "You think this is a"—he added a note of mockery—"secret service problem?"

"I'm here by request," Gudgeon said. "If you want to know what I think, I think there's more important things I could be doing in Ottawa, like making out with my girlfriend."

"So who requested you?"

Gudgeon looked out the window.

Parker spoke, confused, embarrassed. "We did. My boss. I was telling him about the problem, and he pointed out that war criminals might be a touchy subject for a movie. There are a few people in Ontario who don't want the coals raked over. We found that out when the Deschenes Commission, the war criminals inquiry, was sitting in 1985."

"Are you serious? This movie's been made a dozen times already. It's on late-night television."

"Not in Canada," Parker said.

"So who would be uptight about hunting Nazis? Nazis?"

Gudgeon spoke. "A lot of East European groups are always on the watch for any sign of a witch-hunt."

"Is anyone complaining?"

"Not yet. But his boss"—Gudgeon pointed at Parker—"thinks they might. So we were asked to look around. Which I have. And I'm satisfied."

"Have you investigated the people on the set?"

"We've been through the files. We have tabs on a few of them."

"Found out anything I ought to know?" Salter was trying to resist taking Gudgeon, the youthful cold war warrior, seriously, but Ottawa, even Gudgeon, might come up with something helpful. "If you find out something I don't know, tell me, would you? We're on the same side. That the right phrase?"

Gudgeon ignored the sarcasm, looking a little more comfortable at Salter's admission that he might have a legitimate function. He switched to a guardian-of-state-secrets stance. "We see your problem, Staff. We want to help."

"Good."

"Can we count on your cooperation, too?"

"If I hear anyone singing *'Deutschland Über Alles'* in any of the portable toilets, I'll let you know."

Gudgeon put down the paperweight and stood up, shaking the creases out of his trouser legs. He put out his hand to Parker, then to Salter, and left.

Salter and Parker said nothing for a few minutes. Gudgeon had left behind a cloud, a miasma of paranoia with his talk of "keeping tabs" on the whole sleeping population in the name of security.

Salter said, "What the hell did you call those guys in for?"

"You heard. I didn't. My boss did. He likes to share the responsibility."

After a while, Salter said, "I think he's just finishing up his course. This is his end-of-term assignment."

"Did you notice his shoes, by the way? Those brogues with the soles about an inch thick? I didn't think you could buy them anymore. Maybe they're official spook issue."

The atmosphere had largely declined to normal, and Salter got up to go. "I'm sure this thing is personal. If we ever catch the crank, he'll turn out to be some actor getting his revenge on the casting agency for not giving him the part he wanted."

"Keep thinking like that, Charlie."

PART TWO

SEVEN

THE CALL WAS for 9:00 A.M. outside a house in Oakville, the residence (in the script) of Dieter Hauser, the villain being played by Henry Vigor.

As he was getting ready to leave for Oakville, Salter got a call that shooting had been canceled and that there was to be a meeting in Crabtree's office, where his presence was requested.

ONE GLANCE FROM the doorway told him that the film was probably finished. Crabtree, Connor, and Josef Hodek were sitting in a semicircle of chairs facing Diamond, who was leaning back on the couch. Diamond's face had been badly damaged: His forehead and one eye were bandaged, his lip and the corner of his mouth were cut, and one hand was bandaged into a large white paw. "An accident?" Salter asked.

Diamond looked briefly at Salter, then closed his eye. "The wrong line," he said. "Try it again." The cut lip gave him a slight speech impediment.

"Paul got mugged," Crabtree said. "Last night."

"Where? How?"

"On the way home from dinner. He was walking back to his hotel."

"Where?"

"Charles Street."

"How many?"

"Just one," Diamond said, opening his eye and using the opportunity by blinking twenty or thirty times to see if he wanted to leave it open. "What does it matter?"

"If it was only one, it might be personal. Somebody doesn't like you, or didn't last night."

"There was just one. He hit me once." He pointed to his eye. "I got this...and this when I hit the sidewalk. Then he kicked me. Then I got up and hit him. Then we got into a fight."

"How did it start?"

"I was walking along, and this guy bumped into me. I stood aside; then he hit me. I went down, and then I got up and hit him, like I said. After a while, I was winning. Then he ran."

"Updike was right," Connor said. "You can't even get decently mugged in Toronto."

Nobody smiled.

"What did he look like?" Salter asked.

"Young. A kid. Maybe only twenty or twenty-two. Amateur. He was strong, but he wasn't really a fighter."

"Did you hurt him?"

"I think so." Diamond showed his hand. "I caught the side of his face, and I heard something crunch. Then I hit him in the mouth."

"I'll see if we can find him."

"Your guys are already looking. The cops were there in jig time. Somebody must have phoned. Took me to the hospital. No bones broken. I got real good service, I'll say that. Your guys and the people at the hospital couldn't have been better."

"You're a distinguished victim, I guess."

"Not a soul recognized me, or my name. I had to spell it three times. I thought I was the local boy made good. Not one person." Then, in case they thought he was complaining, he added, "You never know, though. Someone once told me that Toronto is the only place where if people recognize an actor on the street, they look away, embarrassed. Michael Caine, I think."

"Did he have an accent?"

"Yeah, British. Cockney. Oh, the mugger. Yeah. He only said a couple of words, but they sounded heavy. European. Otherwise, just your ordinary young white middle-class mugger. He had a tie on. You could call him clean-cut, if you were that kind of writer."

"That a bad area?" Connor asked.

Salter shook his head. "Not west of Bay Street. There are two colleges and a few houses on the street. Nobody makes a living mugging there. It's nowhere near the action. I'll find out what's known."

"We're finished," Josef said. "It will hold us up for weeks. You can't cover it with makeup, and we can't shoot Paul from the neck down."

"It isn't as bad as it looks," Diamond said. "The doctor said the bandages can come off in three days." He was leafing through the script, absorbed in the real world.

Crabtree, who had been looking out the window, silent, now said, "I haven't got three days to spare. We've got to get the Oakville scenes and then the Harbourfront scenes before Vigor's time is up. The rest can wait, but those we have to do. And the boat sequences. I can't do it. Josef's right. I'm finished." It was not said dramatically, and the ordinariness of his tone, the lack of the usual tension in his speech, made him convincing. He was defeated.

No one knew what else to say. They were all involved, but their involvement was nothing compared

to Crabtree's. Salter tried to assess how much he ought
to have foreseen this.

"Write it in," Diamond said without looking up.

They all looked at him, waiting.

"Write it in," he repeated. "The story goes like this:
I see Vigor at the market; then I lose him. A week
later, I see him again, but this time I follow him home
to his house in Oakville. Then I check up on him—
we've shot all that stuff. I find out that he's the guy
I've been looking for, so I go to his house while he's
away and try to find something with his real name on
it. I find the Iron Cross, or whatever it is, in his shirt
drawer."

"It's on the back of the mirror in the bathroom,"
Josef said.

"I changed that. Anyway, when he comes home, he
can tell I've been there, in fact, he sees me waiting in
my car, down the street. Right?"

The others nodded.

"So put some space between the market and the
house search. Find some way Vigor realizes he is being followed and have him find out who I am, then
decide to have me stopped. Two guys take me on—
Charles Street, if you like—but they aren't good
enough, they get interrupted. Whatever. But they leave
me like this. We could take off most of the bandages
for the actual shooting. The script could use a little
juice at this point, anyway."

"It doesn't sound possible," Josef responded, but
the others looked at Crabtree.

Crabtree looked around the group and gave out an
odd little giggle, the noise of a man who has been told
his life savings have been found. "It might work," he
said. "Bill?"

Connor grinned. "We'll blind them with the spray," he said obscurely. "All we need is Henry catching sight of Paul, here, then cut to two guys in sunglasses, one tall and thin, the other short and stocky, beating up Paul on Charles Street. Then have the stunt fella work out a couple of moves for Paul to take them instead. They'll buy that back in St. John."

"Yeah. We'll have to work out something a little better than that. Where's Fisher?" The sap was rising fast again in Crabtree.

"Sulking in his tent," Diamond said.

"Get lost for a while, would you, Paul? Do you mind? Fay, get the car to come and take Paul back to the hotel, and be in Oakville by"—he looked at his watch—"one-thirty. Where's Fisher? Get him here, Fay. Right away. Now let's try out a few ideas before he gets here. Don't go, Charlie. We might need you, depending on how we work it out. Keep Fisher from writing something dumb."

"I want to take care of this assault."

"Later. Paul's all right, and catching a mugger is not important right now."

Diamond went back to his hotel, and Salter found himself in the middle of a script conference, trying to work out a reasonable sequence of fictitious events that would lead to Diamond's mauled face.

WHEN FISHER finally arrived, his opening comment was "Someone need a *writer* on this film?" and Josef put his hand under Salter's elbow and pulled him away to the coffee-making apparatus in the corner of the room. "How are you, Charlie, my friend?" he said as if they had just met on the street. "How is your family? You have a family, of course?"

Salter accepted being led away from the action. "I've got a wife and two kids, Josef."

"A wife. And your two children? Boys or girls?"

The other film men were wrangling hard now. Hodek seemed to be embarrassed by the bad temper that Fisher had generated and to need to create a little peaceful world with Salter in the opposite corner of the room. He repeated his question about Salter's family, but they could not escape the noise of the argument.

Crabtree said, "We've got a crisis. We need a reason Diamond was mugged."

"I could give you twenty," Fisher said. "In the first place, everyone hates the arrogant son of a bitch."

"In the first place, that isn't quite true. I don't. And in the second, I'm not talking about Diamond. I'm talking about the character in the script." Crabtree had already moved into his quiet conversational style, a hairsbreadth away from exploding. "We need a change in the script, your script, Stanley. We've decided that Henry knows he's being followed and does something about it."

"It's there already. I've been stitching it in all along."

"Right. So he has, Jack," Connor said. "Now give us a scene with a reason why Paul should get beaten up between the market scene and the house scenes."

"The simplest way is an accident. Nothing to do with the story."

"Make it part of the story," Connor said. "You can't have the audience worrying about a loose end with ten minutes of the film left."

"You expect me to come up with something just like that?"

"I'm hoping you will, Stanley," Crabtree said. "If not, I'll find someone else who will."

Josef squeezed Salter's arm. "The ballet? How nice to have a boy with talent."

Fisher had finally recognized the deep seriousness of Crabtree's demeanor. "Gimme an hour," he said. "I'll have something in an hour or never." He started to leave the room.

Crabtree looked at his watch. "Eleven o'clock, back here, then."

"If I have anything."

When Fisher had gone, Josef released Salter and joined the film men. "Jack, postpone. This rushing could upset the film."

"Josef, 'postpone' is not an option. As long as I have a chance, I'll be goddamned if I'm going to be one of those guys with seven-eighths of a film in his basement and no chance of raising the money for one ever again. And I'm not letting them take it away from me. I'll finish this thing on time, within the budget. I hope it'll be a good picture, but that's secondary right now. Take a break. Come back at eleven. Fay, get Sherriff, will you. Let's set up this afternoon. Stay here, Bill. Let's go over this again, before Fisher comes back."

Salter saw that Crabtree's new energy had a feverish edge to it and wondered if the high he was getting would be enough to complete the film. For the moment, there was time for Salter to get back to his office, where he arranged to have all the city hospitals checked to see if Diamond's attacker had received treatment at any of them the night before. Then he spoke to the deputy chief about the necessity of having the two valuable people, Diamond and Vigor, guarded. "We ought to have done it before," he said. "They are the most vulnerable spots for anyone who wants to wreck the movie." When that was in place, he drove back to the producer's office to see what the writer had come up with.

Fisher was waiting, sitting on the couch with a handful of sheets of yellow paper. "Here's what I've got," he said. "After Diamond trails Vigor back to his home, we already have a sequence where he looks up the owner of the house in the Oakville town records and finds out who he is, but it isn't the one he's looking for. So he finds out from immigration when this owner arrived in Canada."

"You might have some trouble with that," Salter said.

Fisher looked up wearily. It's bad enough dealing with the morons on the set, his expression said, without having this copper get into the act. "Why?" he asked. "Why will we have trouble?"

"Those records don't exist. The Canadian government didn't keep them. We found out a few years ago that they've been destroyed."

"Bullshit," said Fisher. "Governments don't shred that kind of material."

"Ours did."

"Is this well known, Charlie?" Crabtree asked.

"Everybody who's interested in war criminals knows it. A lot of the people in your audience, I would think."

"Is there no way that you could find out when someone arrived in this country from Europe, back in the fifties?"

"Yes, but it's slow. You go through ships' manifests—is that the term?—the passenger lists. It would take some time."

"That's what we'll do, then. We'll get lucky. We'll stumble across it right away. Okay, Stanley?"

"I guess so." Fisher still looked as if he were surprised that they were bothering to listen to Salter, but he continued. "So then Diamond is seen checking up on this guy, who he finds out was a clerk in the army in Germany, a supplies clerk, something like that, noncombatant, never out of Germany. So he vetted okay for immigration." Fisher looked around the group. "Are you with me?" He looked directly at Salter as some kind of test that he was being understood, even by simpletons. Salter looked at Crabtree, who nodded.

Fisher continued. "Now, the records in Germany will show that this clerk was actually killed in the last few days of the war, in a bombing raid. What happened was that the camp guard, who was already on the run, a well-known criminal, swapped identities with him and after a few years emigrated to Canada as him. We need a scene with Diamond going through the town hall records in this little German town. My idea is that while he's going through the records, some Nazi sympathizer in the office realizes what he is up to, someone who knows who Vigor really is. When Diamond leaves with his information and is on his way back to Canada, ready to confront Vigor, this office guy calls a friend in Canada who calls Vigor and tells him that they are on his trail, and who "they" are, of course. All you need from Henry is him getting a phone call, then making another one asking someone to take care of Diamond."

"It's a bit of a coincidence, with the guy in the office in Germany happening to know about Vigor impersonating a dead man, isn't it?" Connor asked.

They all pondered this for a minute; then Hodek spoke up from the corner. "You might have to add someone else that the clerk tells; then it will be all right. Then the second man can telephone Canada. It works." He turned away and continued with his back to them. "You always know when they are checking up on you, if you have any friends left."

They accepted Josef's authority and moved on. Crabtree said, "Run it past just one more time, Stanley."

Fisher told the story again.

"No," Crabtree said.

"No *what*!" Fisher asked, throwing his paper on the table.

"The idea is right, but you're talking a hundred thousand dollars I haven't got. A crew flying to West Berlin or hiring a German crew. Me paying Diamond for two more weeks. It's a good idea, though. Do it simpler."

"I can't write a story you can make from a piggy bank."

"Three point seven million," Crabtree said. "Cheap, but not a piggy bank."

"We don't need to malarkey around Germany," Connor interrupted. "We just need a shot of Toronto airport with Paul getting on a Lufthansa plane. Then we can dress up a building around here to look like a German town hall. Just the front door. We'll do it mostly inside. Inside it isn't much different from any small-town municipal office, but through the window you can see Bavaria. We don't have to go to Germany.''

"That do?" Crabtree asked Fisher.

"That's the cheap way to do it."

"That's the way we'll do it, then. Now, what about the mugging?"

"I figure we make it a real attempt to kill Diamond," Fisher said. "Two guys, one with a knife. But gallant Paul Diamond holds his own until help arrives, and he is left battered but alive. We'd better find out what kind of fighting Diamond can fake. He'll want to write the scene, anyway, so I won't put too much work on it."

Crabtree looked queryingly at Hodek, who nodded.

"Put the stunt boys on to it," Hodek said. "We'll shoot it from behind, Bill, walking toward his car, something like that, then they jump on him. Afterward, when his face is healed, we'll take a shot of him leaving the building before he walks toward the car."

Crabtree said, "Good. Thanks, Stanley. That's terrific. Where's the casting director? We need an actor to play the German clerk and a location for the government office. And for the fight scene, Fay, get hold of Sherriff, would you? Now let's reschedule."

Fay, who had been trying to speak, said, "You've got to call John Perly. He's in a panic."

"It'll keep."

"No, it won't. He was screaming. He's sitting out at Oakville, waiting."

"Get him, then."

When he had the connection, Crabtree listened for a few minutes, then said, "All over? How many?" A fresh pause, then. "Find someone," he shouted. "Do something. Earn your goddamn pay. Clean it or paint over it. I don't know, but we've just solved a goddamn sight bigger problem than that. We start at one-thirty. Okay?'' He put the phone down.

"That was our set dresser, John Perly,'' he said. "Someone painted swastikas all over the house we're using in Oakville.'' He held up a hand. "Not a fucking word from any of you. We go out there and start at one-thirty.''

Fisher still tried to speak, but Crabtree was gone, through the little gate and down the stairs.

Salter found himself walking down the stairs with Fisher while the others sorted out the problems involved in the changes.

"Swastikas,'' Fisher said, trying to open a conversation.

Salter did not reply.

"What do you think happened to Diamond?'' Fisher asked then.

It was the thing most on Salter's mind. "Somebody with a grudge?'' he said. "Maybe he just got mugged.''

"Got unlucky, you mean.''

Salter nodded. He didn't think so. Everything about the incident sounded amateurish but planned. "You going to eat?'' Salter asked.

Fisher flashed Salter a doubtful look, appraising his entertainment value as someone to spend lunch with. "Not me, thanks. I have to go to work to sort this mess out.''

Now Hodek came down the stairs. Fisher said to Salter, "You know Josef? What's your name again?''

Hodek put his arm around Salter's shoulder. "We are old friends," he said. "And now we shall go to lunch, eh, Charlie? What about you, Stanley?"

Fisher looked slightly disconcerted. Salter watched him recalculate his priorities, trying to assess if Salter and Hodek together constituted a desirable group, and still deciding against it. "I'll catch you guys later," he said. "The best restaurant in the area is Top's. About two blocks down."

How long has Fisher been in the area? Salter wondered. Three weeks? By now Salter had Fisher pegged. After setting aside Fisher's tantrums as normal in the film world, Salter saw Fisher as one of those people who have to be on the inside of everything, preferably at the center. He was the kid who always knew, before they arrived at the summer camp, which counselor's tent was the best one and all the other lore the new boys were ignorant of. Sadly, he was the one in the end who was usually left on his own, in possession of the best spot but unable to find anyone to share it with him. There was just too much of him.

Josef held on to Salter, smiling, waiting for Fisher to go away. Then he turned Salter around and steered him in the opposite direction. "Let's find somewhere quick. I only have half an hour before I must go to Oakville and look at swastikas."

EIGHT

THE HOUSE THAT HAD BEEN found to serve as the home of the character Henry Vigor was playing was one of a dozen "executive mansions," largely inhabited by corporation vice-presidents, on a street near the lake, south of Highway 2. It had required a minimum of set dressing until the swastikas had been painted on.

When Salter arrived, the set was quiet. Everyone was watching a brick-cleaning specialist who had just arrived. The cleaner looked at the swastikas, licked his finger, tasted the paint, and nodded. He said something to the set dresser and began to sort out his equipment.

The set dresser came back to where Salter and Crabtree were watching. "He can get them off," he reported.

There were four signs, two on each side wall, black, about four feet high.

"I ought to have put on a guard, or you should have, but I guess neither of us can know where the bastard will strike next," Crabtree said.

"I've posted bodyguards on Diamond and Vigor. Beyond that, we'd need an army, especially when you're doing the outdoor night scenes."

One of the swastikas was already disappearing.

"Will this put you back?" Salter asked.

"No, it won't."

"Ah, Jack, surely to God. There isn't enough time. We can't make it in three hours," Connor wailed.

Salter realized that Crabtree had been using him to convey his intentions to the director.

Now Crabtree turned on Connor. "You want me to direct the scene?"

"No!" Connor made it sound as if Crabtree had suggested something disgusting. "But you'll only get what you pay for."

"I'm paying two thousand to a lawyer to rent this house for a week. If I had another week, I'd find another two thousand, but I don't." He looked across to where Vigor was sitting on a camp chair, Sherriff in attendance. Diamond was lying on the grass in front of his trailer, his eyes closed. "Now, why don't you run through the scene?"

Connor turned away from him and walked over to Vigor to explain what he wanted.

Salter recruited one of the uniformed policemen to knock on the doors of neighboring homes to see what he could find out. He used his car phone to report the incident to Parker of the Intelligence squad. It was possible that the kind of people who spray-painted swastikas might easily do it the same way twice, even if they had been caught the first time.

When the constable returned, he reported that no one had heard anything during the night except the *Globe and Mail* delivery van.

"A van or a car? By who?" Salter asked.

The man looked puzzled.

"Was it a van like that?" Salter pointed to the cleaning van. "Or a car? What time did it come around? Did more than one hear it?"

The constable went back to his houses.

Across the street, Crabtree was pacing the sidewalk, silently urging everyone to get ready to go back

to work. Connor called across to Sherriff, who patted
Henry Vigor on the shoulder and called out to someone himself. Other voices took up the shout, and the
set came to life.

"Good morning, Charlie." It was Vigor. "Nasty
sight, isn't it?" He pointed to the swastikas.

"I've only seen them in the movies," Salter said.
"More unpleasant for you, I would think."

"You are a privileged generation living in a privileged country," Vigor said. "I got out of Bucharest
just ahead of those gentlemen. I was very low on their
list, but I was on it. Still am, for all I know."

"How did you get away?"

"Egypt first, then Portugal. Then I caught a fishing boat to England, where I spent a year in a camp."

"A concentration camp?"

"No, no, no, an internment camp, in Somerset, a
holiday camp compared to the other kind. One of the
prisoners complained that he didn't like the tooth-
paste. After a year, they let me in to the Pioneer
Corps, without a gun. Filling sandbags, preparing for
the invasion. That dry-cleaned me, and after the war
I became a naturalized citizen and took up my old
trade. I was studying theater, but now if I could make
a living as an actor, that's all I wanted. No more high-
profile jobs, like director, in which I could be accused
of being subversive. A man like Hitler makes you
think he could happen again, tomorrow. Ever since, I
haf been playink Sherman villains." He thickened his
accent for comic effect. "I played some comedy at
first—the English love comic foreigners—but it inter-
fered with my image as a swine, so I had to choose,
and there's more money in villainy. Ironic, isn't it? If
the Iron Guard had caught me, they would have killed

me, and now I spend my time playing their kind." He waved his hand at the cleaning operation. "Do you have a feeling for who is causing the trouble?"

"Louts. Thugs."

"Yes, not very serious, I think. They haven't got the swastikas right. The gentlemen I knew wouldn't have made that mistake."

Salter looked across at the house. "What's wrong with them?"

"They have them all backward. The Third Reich used a swastika with the arms going clockwise. The other way round is an ancient Indian mystical sign of love, I think. God, I hate that sign, even when it is backward. And yet, you know, I have met people from the camps, Jews, who are trying not to hate. Incredible. I was lucky, but I hate. I practice it." Suddenly, he looked at Salter, alarmed. "You *are* Anglo-Saxon, aren't you? Your forebears, I mean?"

"On both sides. My mother came out of a Dr. Barnardo's home, an orphanage."

Vigor settled back in his chair. "I must try to remember I am in Canada, the new melting pot, and not everybody came from England or France. For all I know, your father might have been in the Iron Guard."

They were interrupted by the constable, and Salter took a pace back to listen.

"An Indian family, from India or Sri Lanka, I mean, deliver the *Globe* in a car, sir. But I got two different times. One man says he heard them at three o'clock. Another says they came in a car just after five. She saw them."

"There's a phone in my car. Call the communications desk. Ask them to find out what time the *Globe* is delivered on this street. Then the other time was the swastika painter. Phone that in to the local police and ask them to query all patrol cars in the area at the time. Somebody might have noticed a car. Off you go."

"Will Seth really come with me to get my canoe?" Vigor asked when Salter turned back to him.

"He said he'd be happy to."

"And what can I do for Seth?"

"You could come and watch him dance if you're still here."

"Absolutely right, and we'll all have supper afterward. How nice. I'm sick of eating alone or with Tom Sherriff. When?"

"The week after next. Wednesday." Then, before he could give himself time to think it through, he added, "If it's that bad, come and have dinner with us. At my house."

"Could I really?" Vigor said, turning full face to Salter and smiling. "When?"

"Thursday."

"What time?"

"Seven o'clock."

"Would you tell my driver how to get there?"

"We need you, Henry," Sherriff called through his megaphone.

Helena appeared at the same time. "They are ready, Mr. Vigor," she said, pointing to the house where the swastikas had been cleaned off.

Vigor handed her his cup and flask and pointed toward a chair where his bag lay. "If you would, please, my dear." He walked toward the house.

"No Seth today?" Helena asked Salter as she watched to make sure Vigor didn't lose himself crossing the street.

"They're rehearsing hard now. Not long to go. That was easier to get off than it looked." He nodded toward the house.

She looked at him uncomprehendingly.

"The swastikas. They came off easily. Henry says they weren't real swastikas. Maybe that's why. They aren't very good at their job, these people."

"What are you talking about? Of course they were swastikas."

"Henry says not. The arms were the wrong way round." He drew in the dust with the toe of his shoe. "*That's* a swastika." He scratched again. "Like *that*, it's an Indian mystical symbol of love, Henry says."

She looked at the two symbols for a moment, giggled slightly, and blushed. "What an arsehole," she said in her Oxford accent, giving the vulgarity new life to Salter's ear. "But does that help you?"

Salter had been wondering that himself. He said, "It means that Henry didn't paint them on. He knows what a swastika looks like."

"Helena," Sherriff called. "Down here. Now."

"Ahsewl," Salter said to himself when she was gone, practicing the story he would tell Annie that evening.

THE RESCHEDULING that had been necessitated by Diamond's injuries brought home to Salter something he had half-realized on the first day, that there was no relationship between the time sequence of the completed film and the sequence in which the scenes were shot. Thus, he could get no idea, except from

Crabtree, of how close the producer was to winning his race against his own schedule. From time to time in the next few days, mostly in the end scenes in the harbor, he had a sense, a false sense, that they were nearly there, only to be dislocated again when the next scene they made was a little cameo showing Vigor (in the film) for the first time.

CONNOR CALLED FOR action, and Diamond's car, painted with a sign, J. Syme—Locksmith, rolled to a stop in front of the house. The actor walked smartly through the front gate, nodded to the neighbor, opened a leather tool case, and fiddled with the lock until the door gave. The neighbor nodded back, looked at the sign on Diamond's car, smiled, shook his head, and went back to looking for weeds.

Then they did it six more times because of a second genuine neighbor who appeared in the background, staring and grinning, because of aircraft noise, and because of four other problems Salter couldn't see. He found a tree to lean against as he watched, where he was rejoined by Helena Sukos, who seemed to have adopted him. "Hello again, Mr. Policeman," she said. "Now you have another crime to solve." She pointed toward Diamond.

"Not me," Salter said. "I just advise the script-writer."

"I thought policemen were never off-duty."

"This one is."

"Poor Paul. He is very rude to Fisher, but he is nice to me and the other nobodies. I don't think he is hurt badly, do you?"

"He'll recover. Gives Toronto a bad name, though."

"Who did it, do you think?"

Salter shrugged. "Who knows? How about you? Where were you last night?"

It was a stupid joke, a piece of heavy-handed, faintly sexual horseplay in his role of "policeman," but Helena did not smile.

"I was in bed," she said.

"I was joking. We know it was a man." He patted the girl's shoulder.

She wriggled under his hand. "Don't make jokes like that. Where I come from we don't trust policemen's jokes." She smiled in a formal way. "As a matter of fact, I was having dinner in a very bad restaurant where they served colored food which cost as much as I earn in a week."

"You mean a West Indian restaurant?"

Again he was being stupid.

"No, no. Not soul food. Little strips of yellow vegetables with a slice of green mango and a piece of red pepper all around a little disk of some white fish. And then three spoonfuls of different-colored ices with hot jam on for dessert. Such junk. Afterward I had to have some french fries."

Now Salter wanted to get out of the minefield. He went for the innocuous.

"Maybe you don't like the new cuisine, or whatever it's called. I guess it depends where you're coming from, but Toronto is supposed to have some of the best restaurants on the continent, they tell me."

"You think because I come from Bucharest I don't understand good food?"

Salter blinked. "No, no..."

"Isn't that what you said?"

Salter ran back over his words to find the interpretation. "No, that's just a phrase. It doesn't mean where you come from, but sort of, what your assumptions are, your starting point, like. What do I know about Bucharest? I mean, if you think of restaurants in terms of steak and lobsters, then the one you went to would look pretty bad. See?"

"I think restaurants should serve food, good food, ordinary food, for proper prices, not charge you a hundred dollars and leave you hungry." She seemed quite angry.

"How *was* the food in Bucharest?"

"Bad. We were short of everything. We had line-ups all the time. But I didn't run away to feed my face. I ran to get away from the people who were always watching. I ran away because of the policemen—too many of them." She said this deliberately. "There everyone might be a policeman or spy."

"Here you just have to worry about me and that guy in the secret service." He smiled.

She swung around, confronting him. "No, here I don't have to worry. But that doesn't mean that everything is wonderful here."

"Josef likes it."

She made a face of irritation and disgust. "Josef keeps his real thoughts for his wife. He had a bad time and doesn't want another one. I prefer it here, too, but it isn't black and white, you know. I think sometimes a few shortages would do you all some good." She ended almost talking to herself as she returned to normal.

Salter searched for a change of topic. "How did you get this job?"

"I speak Romanian, and some idiot thought that perhaps that would make Henry Vigor feel at home. I speak German, too, so sometimes, like you, I advise them whenever they have a bit of German in the script. Fisher, the writer, thinks he knows German, but he doesn't."

"Did you ever work on a film before?"

"In Bucharest. Never in Canada. This is a chance for me to learn something."

"How did you leave Romania? Was it hard?" Salter searched for any topic that would relax Helena and keep her around for the rest of the film. He didn't want to alienate her. Nobody else on the set seemed to have time to chat.

She evidently recognized his desire to talk and sat down on one of a pair of canvas chairs. After a moment, she smiled up at him, patted the seat of the other chair, and pulled him down into it. "Sorry, Charlie. You're a nice policeman. I'm being rude." She leaned over and kissed him on the cheek. "Yes, it was quite hard. I was an interpreter. I speak English and German and a little bit of Czech, so I used to take parties of tourists around. And I took Romanians to West Germany and Czechoslovakia for holidays. I always wanted to take a group to England, but I did not have enough clearance yet, and I did not have a family to leave behind to be sure I would go back. But I went to West Germany several times with other guides, all of whom were in the secret police, and after a while they trusted me a bit more, and then they let me go on my own, and the first time they did, I stayed. Then I came to Canada."

Salter changed the subject. "I had lunch with Josef today. He told me all about Prague. You ever been

there?'' He had no idea whether Prague and Bucharest were next to each other or separated by two other
countries. Romania was east of Czechoslovakia,
wasn't it? And where was Hungary? The capital of
Romania is Bucharest, he reminded himself. Budapest is the other one. But where was Bulgaria?

"Oh, yes. I love Prague.''

"You speak Czech, too?''

"A little bit. Enough to be able to guide a tour.''

"Fisher's been to Prague. He speaks Czech, he
says.''

"Ten words. Hello. Good morning. Take me to the
American embassy.''

"Canadian.''

"What?''

"He's Canadian. He would want the Canadian
embassy.''

"But no one would know where the Canadian embassy was.'' She giggled.

"Smart ass.'' He punched her shoulder lightly. "So
I should see Prague, should I?''

"Of course. It was a very sad city then, waiting for
the curtain to go up, but now it would be lovely. It was
very lucky not to be damaged much by the war, so it
is still very beautiful. If I could take you and show
you, you would like it.''

"But you can't.''

"I will wait until the world settles down a bit.''

"Like Josef.''

"Yes.''

"Does that mean you haven't seen your relatives or
friends since you left?''

"No, I saw my sister. We met in West Germany.
This was before the wall came down, but she got per-

mission to travel if she left her husband and three children at home. I hope we can do it every year, but even though she can travel now, it will still be difficult for her to save up enough hard currency. When I am earning more, I can take money for both of us to spend in Germany. Of course, at that time she could not say she was meeting me, and she was terrified that someone might see us and she wouldn't be able to leave again, but now, I guess, she will be all right. I save all my money for our meetings."

"No colored food."

"No colored food, anyway."

"Did you ever know Josef in Prague?"

She looked at him, amazed. "Josef is gone twenty years from Prague. Oh, no. I have met one or two people who Josef knew, working on films. He is a nice man." She made a business of looking around and behind Salter. "Where is Seth? He said he was going to come and watch every chance he got."

"I couldn't wait for him this morning."

"I thought all Canadian boys had their own cars."

"Not Seth. He gets to drive his mother's sometimes, is all. He hasn't got enough money to buy a decent bike."

Why tell her, he wondered. Am I making a point?

"Poor boy. Never mind. Perhaps one day his father will be head of police here."

"I hope not, but you're right. He'll need something like that. Did he tell you he's going to be a dancer. A ballet dancer?"

Helena burst out laughing. "Seth? But none of the swans will be safe."

NINE

THEY WERE interrupted by Henry Vigor, who was having a chair placed for him by the third assistant director. "Charlie," Vigor called. "We went looking for a canoe this morning. Tom took me to some boat shops nearby, but I don't think we saw the right ones. They all seemed rather factory made. What do you think?"

"A canoe's a canoe, right?" Sherriff interjected. "You won't find any better anywhere. Right?"

Salter knew nothing about canoes. He hadn't sat in one for thirty years. But he was aware that there was something of a revival of the old boat-building crafts going on, a revival that had started in the sixties, and he was sure that the individual canoe builders had never entirely disappeared. Besides, he saw no reason to respond to the urgent appeals from Sherriff. In his opinion, Vigor ought to have the full experience of shaking hands with the man who had selected his own cedar and lovingly shaped it with tools handed down by his grandfather and the skills taught him by the Ojibway boyhood companion he had grown up with. Something like that. If keeping Vigor happy was what Sherriff did best, let him earn his money. Then he remembered.

"There's an old guy on the Magnetawan River," he said. "About a hundred and seventy miles north on Highway 69. He builds the best canoes around. He's not on the phone, so you have to drive up and hope to catch him. It's a nice trip. About four hours each way."

Sherriff was looking urgently around him, apparently searching for a rock he could hit Salter with.

"Take me up there, Tom," Vigor said. "There's no shooting scheduled for Saturday. We'll do it then. Thank you, Charlie."

"You're welcome. If he doesn't have one—his boats are often spoken for in advance—there's a place just this side of North Bay. I forget the name, but everybody knows it."

"North Bay is on Highway 11, for Christ's sake," Sherriff said. "It's practically in Quebec."

"That's the place. From the Magnetawan you go on up to Sudbury, just a couple of hours, I would think; then you can go across country and down to North Bay. I don't know how long that takes. A couple of hours, maybe three."

"You're very kind," Vigor said. "Is Seth free on Saturdays?"

"I think he'd love it."

"Why don't you come, too?" Sherriff said. "Or rather, maybe you should take Mr. Vigor."

"Oh, I couldn't get away," Salter said. "I'll ask Seth for you."

He turned back to Helena, but she was gone, needed to set up the next shot, and he strolled over to watch the action.

They were making their sixth attempt to film Diamond breaking into Vigor's home as a voice from near the camera shouted, "Cut."

"Who the hell is giving orders?" Connor asked.

"Sound mixer," the voice said. "I'm not getting a steady pulse."

"What does that mean?"

The sound mixer was apparently seated, bending over his equipment. Salter could not see him for the ring of people who were pressed close around him, now including Connor and Crabtree. Salter moved over to listen.

"It means it won't be in sync," the voice of the mixer said. "And you can't doctor it because it'll be jumping around all over the place."

"How long?" Crabtree demanded. "I mean how long has it been aborting like this?"

"About half an hour, I would guess."

"How come it took so long to find out what was up?"

"I didn't realize what was happening. I think I may have been getting an intermittent signal, and I just caught it."

"What's wrong with the goddamn thing? Can you fix it?"

There was a silence, then the noise of clips being snapped and a metal cover lifted. Then, "There's the problem. That little crystal there, see, in the socket. Someone's been messing about with it. Taken a screwdriver to the socket, it looks like."

"Can you fix it?"

"We'll need a new crystal."

"Will someone in town have a stock?"

"Sure. I'll write out what we want, and you can send a driver in."

"No," Crabtree said. "Use the phone. Do it yourself, Joe. Tell them to put it in a cab, now. We'll save half an hour on the journey."

Salter, reminding himself he was supposed to be just an adviser, asked, "You want me to get an investigator?"

"We haven't got time now." Crabtree didn't even look at Salter. "Wait until the shooting's over. Joe, how long before we can start?"

"Half an hour after it gets here. We'll have to test it."

Crabtree looked at the sky, then at his watch, finally at a sheet of paper he carried on a clipboard. "Let's take a break, then. Call in an hour. I guess we're lucky you caught it. We could have wasted the whole day."

Salter went back to join Vigor, who was sipping the brown liquid from his flask.

"What is this Oakville, Charlie?" Vigor asked. He had an air of serenity appropriate to a nobleman of another age whose carriage has broken down and who was now sipping the local wine in the courtyard of the inn while the peasants toiled to repair the damage.

"It's a rich suburb. It was a town on its own once, but you'd have trouble finding much open country between here and Toronto nowadays. Place is full of brewery executives. Used to have the highest per capita income in Canada, but it's slipped a bit lately."

"I've done well, haven't I?"

Salter understood the pronoun to refer to the fictional character Vigor was playing. "What exactly have you been doing? How did you get to be rich?"

"That's all very vague. I own some sort of manufactory, I think. Nothing like that is important in a thriller. I drive a Mercedes, and I own a house. That's enough."

"Helena says you're from her hometown. The real you, I mean."

Vigor laughed. "What a funny way to describe Bucharest. Yes. It was nice to find someone on the set from there, but I haven't seen it for fifty years, of course. She tried to tell me what had changed, but we don't speak the same language."

"Romanian?"

"No, no. No, I haven't forgotten that. I meant politically. She's a child. All she knows is the socialist East and the decadent West. I'd like to say I have no politics, but it's difficult to forget. Helena is violently antisocialist, but she doesn't like the West much, either. But I remember 1940 and the years before. I've been lucky, Charlie. I was a Communist then, and I got out before the Fascists found me. It was obvious to me from 1933 where the real danger lay, and I must say, when I got to England, I still thought the hope lay with Moscow, and I was surprised that not all of the English felt the same way. They were right, of course, and I changed when that god failed me as well as others. I'm grateful to be where I am now, with a government that puts my teeth on edge but doesn't knock my door down in the middle of the night and drag me off to a stalag or a gulag." Vigor took a sip of his drink. "Totalitarianism has been a lot slower coming to the West than Orwell predicted," he ended. Now he looked at Salter as if he expected a response, but Salter had nothing to say.

"I like what I've seen of Canada," Vigor added courteously. "If I were younger..." His voice trailed off as he lost interest in what he was saying. He looked around. "Tom," he called sharply. "Tom, what's happening?"

"They're just wrapping up the break-in scene, Henry."

"How much longer? Find out, will you?"

As Sherriff trotted off, Vigor turned back to Salter. "And you, Charlie? Tell me about yourself. Do you have any other children?"

"I've got another boy."

"Policeman?"

"No, he's in business school."

"What's that?"

"It's a course. Some kind of degree. I don't know, to tell you the truth."

They were interrupted again by Sherriff. "It'll be at least three hours, Henry. We have to finish the scene of Diamond searching the house. Then the shot of him driving away. After that, you come on."

Vigor stood up. "Let's go and have some tea, Tom. Take me to that nice coffee shop in the hotel."

"The Courtyard? In Toronto?"

"That's the place. We've got three hours to dispose of. Won't you come, Charlie? We could talk about the ballet."

"Sorry, I have to stick around. Ask me again, though. I've never been in that coffee shop."

Vigor walked off with Sherriff, and Salter went for a stroll along the line of Winnebagos.

A man was sitting on the steps of the makeup truck. He looked about eighty years old and in poor shape. One eye was obliterated by scar tissue, and another scar ran down his cheek. His teeth, when he smiled at Salter, were appalling—yellow and black, twisted and broken.

"Hi," he said. It was Ranovic.

"What the hell."

"Derek had some time on his hands, so I let him practice on me." He looked around to see if they were alone. "Good, isn't he?"

"A magician. Pity he couldn't find you a hunch-back, though." Now Salter looked around, more conscious of feeling foolish by humoring Ranovic than concerned about damaging Ranovic's cover.

"They nearly finished?" Ranovic asked.

"Who knows? I can't even tell who's in charge."

"The Newfie with the fringe around his chin. As long as he's talking, something might happen."

"We okay here?" Salter asked, meaning, Can we talk?

"Unless that spook has got this tree bugged."

Salter sat down on the grass beside Ranovic. "What happened to Diamond? What's the gossip?"

"You want it all?" Ranovic laughed. "Okay, he's gay. Got beaten up for propositioning the wrong guy. Won't admit it."

"He's not gay. What else?"

"No? These are the drivers talking. Then he was screwing around with someone's girl. The star taking his pick of the groupies."

"These the same guys talking?"

"The same guys, but a different segment. Or it's union trouble."

"What else?"

"One of the guys thinks we've got a Nazi on the set."

"I doubt it. Any others?"

"You want to know what I think? I think this is one of those things where you've got a little bit of trouble which starts a fire but it isn't necessarily connected. It started with the alarm, then some other clown put in the police call, then there was the sprinklers, and now the cameras. In the meantime, someone took a poke at Diamond to see if he could fight and found out he could. This is very high-tension work. There are a lot of grudges around when a film's nearly finished, Derek says. It'll go away. But Diamond has played a few tough-guy parts, and I think some character got drinking and starting to wonder how tough he really was. Like taking on James Bond to see what he's made of when he's not on a movie lot. One of the bit players says that guys like Diamond are always being challenged in L.A.''

"So I should relax? It's all just a brushfire?''

"I think so.''

"I don't know.'' Salter felt someone else approaching and got to his feet. "So that's it,'' he said loudly. "You drive the truck on to the site, then sit around all day. Nice work.''

"That's right. Nearly as soft as your job. But we only get paid when we work. You guys are on salary for life unless they catch you on the take. When was the last time you heard of a cop being fired because he wasn't any good? It's like the army.''

Salter walked away trying to look sour.

As HE WATCHED Hodek discuss the scene with the cameraman, Salter realized something that had not registered before: that he couldn't understand what they were saying. By now he was so used to overhearing Helena and Henry Vigor chatting in Romanian and Hodek teasing Helena in Czech, as well as hearing the carpenters build the sets in Italian, that he had developed a blind ear, as in a foreign land, but this was a language he recognized without understanding it.

When Hodek was finished setting up the scene, Salter made his way to him.

"Your cameraman French?"

"From Quebec. His name is Paul Tessier. I will introduce you."

"No need. Doesn't he speak English?"

Hodek looked whimsical. "Better than I do, Charlie, but he insists on using French."

"So you have to translate for everybody?"

"For all the Canadians. Helena helps out. She speaks French, too, and Tessier is teaching her about cameras. But it's no problem. I am the one who gives him his orders."

"Is he that good?"

"He is the best. That's why he can refuse to speak English."

"Handy for us to have some foreigners around, isn't it, so we can talk to each other." Salter left him there, but afterward he watched Tessier whenever he was nearby, and he never saw him break down. Whenever he was addressed in English, he simply looked polite and called for Hodek. Salter fantasized coming up behind him and saying something like "Your wife is back" to test him, but he never did. Certainly, for everyday purposes, Tessier had trained himself as well as if he were a spy.

Finally, Hodek got the lighting set, and they prepared to shoot the interior scenes of Diamond searching the house. Salter decided that this was a good time to find out how the bits and pieces of research were going.

Thirty-five minutes later, he was talking to Sergeant Parker of the Intelligence unit.

TEN

"WE'VE DONE A computer check," Parker said. "We haven't found anything. One of the drivers did a month for drunk driving last year. So did Crabtree, the producer. One of the actors was fined for possession of marijuana. That's it for the Canadians. We've put a query in to L.A., where Diamond and Fisher live. They said they'd try and find out if the two of them had squared off against each other in the past. Would it help if they found something?"

"Not that I can see. Just make it harder to think about."

"Maybe the CSIS guy will come up with something."

"Will he tell us if he does?"

"You'd better talk to him. He's using an office upstairs."

SALTER WALKED INTO Gudgeon's temporary office and made an effort to be agreeable. "Hi, there," he said.

"How are you, Staff?" Gudgeon caught Salter's hand in an elaborate entwining grip, making Salter wonder if he was getting a signal.

"What's the word from MI5, or whatever the Ottawa equivalent is?" Salter asked.

Gudgeon chuckled. "I guess I'm your first spook, eh, Staff?"

"I never believed in you."

"We exist, all right. Let's see. What do I have for you?" He made a show of mentally selecting the information that Salter might be allowed to hear. "We still haven't seen any sign of a serious right-wing involvement."

"What about the left? You watch them, too. You used to."

"We monitor any security-threatening activity."

"Found any Bolsheviks?"

"I see you're being ironical, Staff. I can understand that. But ever since Gouzenko, we've— But that's for another time."

Salter couldn't resist. "Gouzenko happened before you were born. And he's dead. Are people still trying to make contact with him? From the other side?" Spooks? he thought.

Gudgeon smiled, showing he caught the joke. He continued. "Look at the U.K., Staff. They're still finding guys who were planted in the thirties."

"So what are you doing?"

"You've got a few people who we're getting a reading on."

"Who?"

"Hodek, your photographer, for one."

"He fled the Russians in 1968. He must hate them."

"It was a great cover for their organization. It was easy to plant a few people among the refugees. We're trying to find out what he was doing before '68. Who was he?"

"He was a filmmaker." Intrigued now, Salter asked, "How will you find out? You can't ask the old Czech government, can you?"

"We have people in place we can ask."

"Canada has moles? I don't believe it."

The coach looked as if one of his players had accused him of never having personally scored a goal in
his life. "Never mind that," he said, trying for authority. "Now, the actor who's playing the villain,
Henry Vigor."

"He left Romania in 1940. To escape the Nazis,"
Salter said.

"We believe that."

"He's lived in England ever since."

"We know that. The point is he could be on the Iron
Guard's hit list. We think some of those guys may still
be around. We'd like to smoke 'em out."

"Who are the Iron Guard? Hitler's old age pen-
sioners?"

"They're Romanian. They go back to the thirties."

"I thought you had tabs on everybody."

"I can't go into details. There's a Hungarian on the
lighting crew. He looks clean. That's about it. And
we're having a look at the cameraman, Tessier. He's
from Quebec. He's been in the separatist movement
since his student days. Probably still hates the An-
glos."

"He didn't mug Diamond, and he couldn't have
switched on the sprinklers, and whoever made the
phone calls didn't have a French accent. And I doubt
he's got an accomplice, because there aren't any other
Frenchmen on the set, and he refuses to speak English. Have a word with him yourself. I imagine you'd
have to speak French in your job. And Gudgeon is
French, isn't it?"

"No, it isn't. My family came from the States after
the Revolution. Loyalists. I'm learning French at night
school. That's it, then."

"You've missed two."

"I don't think so. Who are they?"

"There's a guy named Ranovic. He's another of these Bohemians. Yugoslavian, I think. I wouldn't trust him."

"We checked him. We know who he is." Gudgeon looked at Salter with hate. "Who's the other?"

"Helena Sukos, the fourth A.D. She says she's Romanian, escaped to the West. I have my doubts."

"Why?"

"She's very contemptuous of capitalist food. Thinks we're disgusting. Don't write that down. I'm just joking."

"We're not. There's nothing on her."

Salter felt the ground give way under his feet once more. As a policeman, he was familiar with the amount of covert, illegal surveillance that was constantly going on in the war against urban crime—the squads of undercover men, the wiretapping, and all the rest of it—but this naive security agent was making him feel how innocent he was, that "out there" you had to believe that endless inquiries were going on, a huge activity of notes being taken and files created. It had to be, because security operations were a self-fulfilling prophecy. Once you had hired enough Gudgeons, what else could they do except justify their existence? And this was in Canada. What must it be like elsewhere? He remembered reading somewhere about a man under suspicion in a Czech jail who was questioned constantly by ever-changing teams of interrogators. He never broke down because he knew nothing; though he wanted to confess, he could never find out what they wanted to know. When he eventually got out of jail, he learned that he had been used for training purposes by apprentice interrogators learning their trade, like a charity patient in a teaching hospital.

Salter lost the urge to make fun of Gudgeon. "You will let me know if you find out anything that might help me?" he asked as he stood up.

"No question. And call me anytime." He gave Salter his card. "Don't leave that lying around, will you."

"I'll memorize the number and eat it."

WHEN HE GOT BACK to Oakville, the interior scene was finished, and the crew was finally setting up for the arrival home of Vigor. The script called for Vigor to pull into the alley behind the house and to be waylaid by the same grass-cutting neighbor who had been successfully fooled by Paul Diamond's locksmith cover.

The neighbor chats with Vigor about the problem that Vigor must have had to make him send for a locksmith. Vigor acts instinctively to get rid of the neighbor by acknowledging the problem with the lock, then walks around the house, apparently to examine the new lock but in fact to check through the windows that there is no one still inside. Then he goes inside and starts to pack, first arming himself with a pistol that he retrieves from a drain in the basement.

In fifteen attempts they got as far as Vigor being intercepted by the neighbor. Then it started to rain, making further filming impossible. They would have to reschedule, if possible, for the next day. The crew began to pack up, and Salter found himself with an arm about his shoulders.

"My friend Charlie," Hodek said. "Have you caught him yet? The mugger?"

"Nope. And we probably won't. He didn't check into any hospital in Metro."

"Another day behind. I don't think we can finish in time."

"The shoestring's only so long," another voice said. "How are you, Josef?" It was Fisher, the writer.

"Stanley, do we need the next sequence?" It was Crabtree. "Couldn't we cut to Henry arriving at the dock, with Paul right up his ass?"

"No way. You've got to establish that scene at the dock," Fisher said. "I've structured it as a cat-and-mouse sequence. Diamond is waiting for Vigor out in the car. Inside, Vigor has seen him but figures out how to get clear. When he runs, he has about a twenty-second lead. Besides, the way I've got Vigor getting clear is neat. One of the best scenes."

"Maybe yes, maybe no," Crabtree said. "We may have to cut it down to just the chase, and only a bit of that. I could probably save a day that way. I need it."

Fisher went berserk. "You're turning this into a goddamn roadrunner cartoon," he screamed. "All cars and guns. I'm not having this scene *touched*."

Fisher had chosen a bad moment to defend his script. Crabtree said to Connor, "Cut it."

Connor said, "Jesus, Jack..."

Crabtree said, "Cut the whole sequence. Go from finding the Iron Cross to arriving at the dock."

Fisher said, "I'll blow this right out of the water."

Crabtree said, "That's the third time you've said that. Now you have time to do it. Get off the set. Get off the set, Stanley, and don't come back, ever."

Fisher looked around, apparently searching for something to hit Crabtree with, and the producer waved to a security guard, who came trotting over.

"Escort this guy off the set," Crabtree said. "If he comes back, have him arrested." He turned away.

For a few moments, Salter felt sorry for Fisher, getting some feeling for what it must have been like to see a man declared an outlaw. Fisher looked around at the faces that were watching his, more or less covertly, said to the security guard, "Don't touch me, buddy," and walked off to the parking lot.

"OKAY, let's go back to the office. Tom, call them for ten tomorrow. We'll do the fight scene on Friday. The Harbourfront stuff is a night scene. We shoot that at four o'clock Sunday morning."

As Vigor was leaving, he called to Salter, "Don't forget to ask Seth if he would come with us on Saturday."

"I'll tell him."

When all the others had gone, Salter turned to Hodek. "So who could have damaged the sound recorder, Josef? It had to be someone who knew how it worked, didn't it? Who knows about that around here except the sound man?"

"Me," Hodek said immediately. "Paul Tessier, Bill Connor. Bill used to be a photographer."

"Or someone we don't know about. I mean, someone we don't know has experience with sound equipment."

"It must be. I will vouch for Paul, and it was surely not Bill." Hodek shook his head. "Another day behind. I don't think there is much time left."

AT HOME THAT EVENING Salter relayed the message from Vigor to his son.

"Sure," Seth said. "Terrific. I'll find out where the best places to go are."

Salter told him about the canoe builder on the Magnetawan River and settled down to read the script once more. He wanted to see if he could anticipate any security problems. A lot of the remaining scenes took place at night, near or on the water, and Salter decided that there weren't enough guards to keep the set secure in the dark. The area needed to be searched at dusk, then cordoned off. Twenty more men for as long as it took.

In the course of his reading, he came across the scene of Vigor's escape from the Oakville house, the scene Fisher was so proud of.

As Fisher had written the scene, Vigor escaped from the back of the house, knowing that Diamond was watching the front by the trick of calling for an airport limousine, loading in his bags, then driving away from his garage at the back of the house.

What bullshit, Salter thought before he realized he was making the mistake of treating the story as if it described a real police trap. The incompetence of the character being played by Diamond and the certainty that Vigor would get away were irrelevant. What mattered was the little trick that Vigor pulled and then a squeal of tires and a flurry of cars taking off after him. If you lived along the lakeshore near Oakville, you could see what rubbish it was, but Fisher was working on his memories of twenty years before. He had not bothered to get the local geography right just to keep a few natives happy.

Salter the movie producer read it again. That'll do, he thought. That'll work.

ELEVEN

By THE TIME Salter arrived, the fire was under control, although smoke continued to billow up into the dawn sky. Crabtree's office and the copy shop at the end of the corridor had been destroyed, but the first floor was still intact.

Crabtree was there with Carole Banjani, who seemed to be acting as his attendant, ministering to him as he stared, silent and unmoving, at the ruins of his office.

Salter asked, "How serious is it, Jack?"

Carole Banjani tried to wave Salter away, but Crabtree turned and focused on him. "If I find them, I'll kill them," he said.

"Could it have been an accident caused by one of the derelicts around here?"

Now the fire marshal approached. "The front door was forced, as was the door of Balmuto Productions. Someone scattered a lot of paper around, then set fire to some oil-soaked rags."

"Was the film in there?" Salter asked.

Crabtree nodded. "The print. I'll have to get another set."

Salter said, "Where is the original?"

"The negatives? In the lab. In the vaults."

Banjani said over her shoulder as she clutched Crabtree's arm, "You don't think the negative is stored in some wooden fire station, do you?"

"So why burn down your office?"

Crabtree said, "Why beat up Paul? Why paint swastikas all over the house in Oakville? Why do any of it? Because every little helps, I guess. They're looking for the last straw, the one that will break my back, so find them, Charlie, before they find it."

Carole Banjani pulled on his arm, and he allowed himself to be led back to his car. Salter walked along the street to the café where he had drunk coffee with Crabtree and ordered some pancakes and bacon. It was still only seven o'clock, and it was going to be a long day.

SOMEONE WAS WAITING for him when he reached his office. The constable on the front desk called to him as he was putting in his security card to open the door to the elevators. Salter turned to find a man in his early forties dressed like a banker and carrying a large suede document case under his arm. He offered Salter his card, which read Porter Williams. There was no other identification. Salter waited. The man was too prosperous looking to be selling anything. Salter turned the card over and handed it back. "Did we have an appointment?" he asked.

"I'd like to make one, Staff Inspector, but I'd prefer it if you could give me a few minutes now." He sniffed the air. "Smoke?"

"There was a fire. What do you want to see me about?" Salter heard a small alarm ringing. This wasn't a man to hang around outer offices on the chance of catching people.

"I represent some people with an interest in the film you are advising on. Where was the fire?"

Nothing personal, then. A money man of some kind. No need to be too respectful. He had no right to

Salter's time. But better talk to him. Salter by now was feeling more than a little protective about the film.

"Jack Crabtree knows I'm here," Williams said.

"When did you talk to him?"

"Yesterday."

Ah. Salter signed the man in and took him up to the office. On the way he said, "The fire was in Jack Crabtree's office."

"What was damaged?"

"Crabtree's office. The film is still in the lab."

Williams absorbed this, then took his time about making himself comfortable in the visitor's chair. He looked at Salter as if expecting the policeman to know what he wanted to hear. Salter recognized the technique and waited. Eventually, Williams said, "There have been a few other problems, I hear."

Salter said, "Tell me first. Who are you? Who do you represent? And what does Crabtree want me to tell you?" Salter wanted this man out of his office. After arson, what? He was trying to decide whether it was necessary to put personal guards on Crabtree or Connor or Hodek. How many?

Williams resettled himself. "Do you know anything about film financing, Inspector?"

"I know they cost a lot of money and someone has to put up the money. Dentists, Jack says. That you? You one of the dentists?"

Williams smiled. "Not quite."

Salter waited some more.

"I do represent them in a way."

"What way is that?" Now Salter felt he had a line on Williams. The man was a lawyer, a rich lawyer from one of those firms with three Anglo-Saxon partners and a Ukrainian one to get the ethnic trade. Formidable in court, but this was Salter's turf.

"Let me explain." Some of the purring note left his voice as Williams got to the point. "The dentists, as you call them, put up the money. Then they insure themselves."

"You're an insurance agent?"

"I work for them. I'm a guarantor. I guarantee, or my employers do, that the film will get made."

Salter thought about this. "Let me try this out. First someone puts up the money; then he insures himself against losing it."

"Against losing all of it."

"That's you doing the insuring."

"There may be other intermediaries involved, but that's essentially it."

Salter was interested now. "How do you guarantee it? I mean, what do you actually do?"

"If necessary, we finish the film."

"How? What if something happens so that no one can finish it? If the leading actors get into an accident?"

"Then we finish it in another way."

"But what's the point? You may ruin it so that no one will show it."

"It's still a tax write-off. An unfinished film isn't."

"Even if it's a pile of junk?"

"My clients would still have fulfilled the requirements of the Tax Act. That's the way the capital cost allowance works in film investment."

"So you can just walk in and take it away from Crabtree?"

"We've only done that once."

"But you'd try and finish it properly."

"Of course. There may be ways of recovering some of the costs. Video rentals.''

"At what point do you move in?"

"Call it the point of no return.''

Now Salter thought he understood what Williams wanted to know, and he couldn't resist saying it. "You want me to help you decide if we've reached that point?'' Screw you, buddy.

But Williams was ahead of him. "All I'd like is your assessment of the criminal activity that seems to be taking place.''

"This is the police you're talking to. We run our investigations our way.''

"I'm aware of that. And I'm aware that you really are investigating this problem, not just advising. Nevertheless, Jack Crabtree thought you might be able to reassure me.''

So there it was. Salter's instincts were to send Williams packing, a response that grew out of his protective feeling about the film. But it seemed he might be able to do more good for Crabtree by talking to Williams.

"My sergeant is waving at me through the glass. Let me deal with him and then we won't be interrupted.''

Salter left the office and called Crabtree at his home. Crabtree assured him that Salter should talk to Williams. "I put him on to you,'' Crabtree said. "I had no choice.''

"I haven't seen him around before. How did he know of the problem?''

"He's got a guy on the set all the time. You've seen him. He's generally in my office studying the shooting schedule. But Williams has been talking to someone else. He knows more than this guy could tell him.

But he wouldn't tell me who, and I can't press him without sounding worried, and I was trying to be very lighthearted about it to him. You think he's happy now?"

"I don't know how you can tell with a guy like that. I'll do my best."

Salter returned to the office. "What do you want to know?" he asked Williams.

Williams looked at Salter in a way to let Salter know that he knew he had been checked up on. Tolerantly. Then he began. "In your judgment, do these incidents constitute an ongoing threat to the film's production schedule, and can you contain them?"

"You mean, is it just a nuisance, or could it escalate until it wrecks the film? I don't know. At first, I thought it was just a nuisance, but not anymore. Beating up Diamond and setting fire to a building are serious and difficult to guard against. There must be fifty different ways to do damage if you're allowed on the set, and it looks as if that's where it comes from. It's the threat to people I'm most concerned with. We've got the leading actors under protection."

"I know. That's the chief worry, of course. Everybody else is replaceable. But what's your thinking on the why of it?"

Salter pondered this one. Did Crabtree know that Williams regarded him as replaceable? He had no doubt that Williams was double-thinking, even triple-thinking him. The question wasn't about what Salter was thinking, he was certain. Williams wanted to know what kind of thinking he was capable of. At the least, he wanted to know if Salter was doing his job. "I understand you're in touch with Jack Crabtree," he countered. "And you've got a man on the set you are talking to. Anyone else?"

"How do you mean?"

"Have you got anyone else on the set reporting back to you?"

"What makes you think that?"

"It's what I would do if I were you. Pay someone to tell me the rumors, the gossip, stuff your man wouldn't hear."

"Why?"

Patiently, Salter told Williams what the guarantor pretended not to know. "Everything adds up to an attack on Crabtree, or could. It might help to find out who has a grudge against him. The only person who'll really be hurt if the picture stops is Crabtree."

"And Fisher, I suppose. He's got a financial interest."

Salter said, "How far are you prepared to let Crabtree go in the hole?"

Williams ignored the question. "Do you plan to increase the security?"

"I plan to make the rest of the time on the set as secure as we can, but we have to hope we get lucky. Assassinating someone is easy if you don't mind getting caught."

Williams said nothing, and Salter thought he now saw what his real concern was. "You guarantee the film, no matter what?"

"We don't have a limiting clause. But we, too, insure ourselves against most things."

Salter opened his mouth to speak and then laughed. "You could jerk me all around the block on this one, couldn't you?"

Williams made a self-deprecating gesture and stood up.

"Tell me this," Salter continued. "Is there any way you or the people you represent could get hurt? You sound as though you've got it all sewed up."

Now Williams smiled slightly, unable to resist the flattery.

Salter stood up and clipped his pen inside his jacket. "I guess it's what comes of having the money in the first place," he said, moving around the desk to walk to the door with Williams. "Like a bank. You read about all these debts they can't collect from the Third World, and yet they still don't collapse, and you realize that however incompetent and greedy they've been, they can't lose. Are you like that?"

Williams nodded, unruffled by Salter's rudeness. "More or less," he said. "Let me think. If it cost much too much money to complete the film, that could hurt us."

"But not kill you."

"Oh, no. But let's go one step at a time." Williams tucked the suede envelope under his arm and moved to the door. "A lawyer would tell you that my interest in this movie is a legal one and gives me certain rights," he said.

Salter cut him off. "You won't need a lawyer. Crabtree will keep you in touch, I'm sure. If you have any doubts, call me."

"Thank you."

Williams offered his hand and withdrew it almost in the same moment so that the contact was as small as possible consistent with the gesture having taken place at all. It was like saying good-bye to a royal duke.

THAT NIGHT, Vigor came to dinner. The investigation into the fire had had no immediate results, and Crabtree had confirmed that though his records had suffered, the film had not, so Salter left them to it, knowing what kind of panic Vigor's visit was likely to be generating at his house.

Even Seth was worrying. "Shouldn't we have champagne?" he asked, and, "What are you going to cook—not our ordinary stuff?"

Annie had spent the morning trying to figure out what would be a treat for a Romanian Englishman who probably lived on blintzes filled with caviar, lost her nerve several times, then, deciding that life would go on no matter what she did, finally poached a salmon, boiled some new potatoes, got a bunch of asparagus ready for the microwave, and sliced up some tomatoes and avocado, over which she poured some oil and vinegar. Dessert was raspberries from the canes at the end of the yard. At the last minute, because it didn't look enough, she added a slab of Cambozola. She assembled the food in the kitchen, looked it over, said (to herself), "Fuck it," and turned her attention to cleaning up the eating area in the backyard.

Salter called in at the liquor store and bought vodka, gin, white wine, cognac, and sherry. (He had whiskey.)

Vigor arrived exactly on time, bearing flowers and a can of peanuts, escorted by his police bodyguard, who agreed that the actor was in good hands and took the rest of the evening off. Vigor was dressed in a Hawaiian shirt and pink trousers, and Salter hurriedly buried his jacket and tie as he saw him coming up the path.

As soon as they had all shaken hands, he took Vigor out to the patio and asked for drink orders. "Rye whiskey, please," Vigor said. "I've never had it, and it is the local wine, isn't it?"

When Salter served the drinks, they raised their glasses ceremoniously for the first sip. Vigor tasted, looked thoughtfully at his glass, and said, "I'm glad to have tried it. Do you think I could have some more water in it?"

Seth tripped over his chair as he ran to get the water. They all laughed, and the ice was broken.

Vigor ate everything, seeming to like the boiled potatoes most of all. Annie poured coffee and set out the brandy, and Vigor talked. For two hours he told stories about his career, about the parts he had played, the famous he had played against, and the places he had been. Seth, who knew all of his thriller movies, prompted him from time to time, totally hypnotized by the old man, while Salter and Annie watched and listened. Periodically, the doorbell rang, and Seth raced to answer it, returning each time with a gesture indicating that it was no one they need bother about. (He confessed later that he had told all his friends to drop by and look at Vigor.)

Then, at ten o'clock, Vigor said, "That's enough for me. Now let's hear from Seth. Go and get *The Tempest*, Seth."

Seth looked quickly at both his parents and disappeared. Annie went off to make some more coffee, and Salter tried to fill in the gap until Seth reappeared with a giant volume of the complete Shakespeare.

"Seth's been keeping me from boredom," Vigor said. "Off you go, Seth: 'Our revels now are ended.'"

He turned to Annie. "Not very appropriate for his age, but we've been doing the stuff I remember."

Slowly, carefully, without mistakes, Seth picked his way through Prospero's speech.

"Not bad, is he?" Vigor said. "Now..."

"I don't want to do any more," Seth said, and put the book on the floor.

"Now you read it," Annie said.

"I don't have to *read* it, my dear," and Vigor performed the lines, looking out over the garden, ending with a quietness that could not suffer an encore.

AFTERWARD, when Vigor had gone, Seth said, "He makes it sound as if he *wrote* it."

ON FRIDAY, Salter watched them film the fight scene. They rehearsed all day in the studio; then, at dusk, they moved to a location on a side road off King Street East, a warehouse district where the commercial activity had ended for the day.

It was delicately orchestrated. Diamond did his stuff, breaking a finger here, kicking a scrotum there, but going down slowly until the muggers were interrupted by an actor playing a security guard. The thugs ran off, and Diamond, bloody and on his knees, was still alive.

Salter was impressed. Even through the theatrics it was obvious that Diamond knew something about street fighting, and he seemed to be in excellent condition. Fighting, even for cameras, is exhausting work, but Diamond had some breath left.

TWELVE

On Saturday, Seth went with Vigor to look for his canoe. He came home long after supper. "We got one," he cried as he came through the door.

Salter asked, "From the guy on the Magnetawan River?"

"No. I remembered there was a man built canoes who has a place on the highway, just outside Huntsville, on the way to Algonquin Park. A bunch of the camp counselors stopped there once to watch him work."

"Did he have one?"

"Not that wasn't spoken for. So we went up to that terrific place you told Mr. Vigor about near North Bay, and they had one. They were supposed to be closed, but Tom Sherriff talked the guy into letting us in, and then he gave us a tour of the factory."

"I imagine Sherriff used the name of Henry Vigor, the famous movie actor."

"I guess. I'm starving, Mom."

"It's chili," Annie said. "I mean, that's what there is."

"Great." Seth sat square to the table and waited to be waited on. "You should see this place, Dad. The two guys who run it are brothers, I think. Anyway, they've had it a long time. They build everything to order. God, they're terrific. Most of the boats are for fishing, from sixteen feet up, to take an outboard up to forty horse, the guy said. But he had a couple of canoes, so Henry picked one, and then he made the guy explain how he built it. Henry's practically an expert himself now."

Annie arrived with the chili and a plate of toast. Seth continued: "How about going fishing sometime, Dad? We never do stuff like that. If we bought one of these boats, we could put it on a boat trailer. Go anywhere. Couldn't we? You could teach me to tie flies and stuff. One of those rites of passage fathers and sons do together."

Salter said, "Henry enjoy himself?" He could always come back to Seth's request later if Annie assured him that Seth wasn't just entertaining himself with a fancy again.

"I'll say. He made us take a detour just past Huntsville so he could go down some back roads. He was really turned on by the scenery, the lakes and stuff. He kept saying, " 'Everybody goes to Niagara Falls, but this is the part that nobody sees.' "

"What time did you start?"

"Nine o'clock this morning. Mr. Sherriff drove us. He drives *fast*."

"What time did you leave North Bay?"

"Around four. Then we screamed home in about three and a half hours."

"Didn't you stop to eat anywhere?" Annie asked.

"No, we had these terrific picnic lunches that Mr. Vigor got from the Danish Food Center, so we didn't have to stop at all. He really kept us moving," Seth said, adding, "Mr. Vigor said he would come to watch the show."

"Sherriff, too?"

"I doubt it. He didn't say anything. All he did was make phone calls. Every place we stopped he made about fifty phone calls."

"Ten hours in a car is a bit much. Were you sorry you went?"

"Oh, no. Mr. Sherriff did all the driving, and I sat in the back and sort of rehearsed."

"Rehearsed what?"

Now Seth looked diffident, embarrassed. "He'd brought two copies of a play along, and we read bits from it. One bit, really, over and over."

They looked at him, waiting for more.

"It was *Henry IV, Part I*. He explained the play to me; then we rehearsed the scene where the King is talking to Prince Hal, kind of jerking him around. I played Hal."

"Fun?"

"Hard work. Hard as dancing. But yeah, it was terrific. We did it about twelve times. I practically know it by heart."

"And Sherriff had to listen to this all day?"

"Till we left North Bay. Then Henry fell asleep, and Tom put on the radio."

"Remind me never to offer you two a ride," Salter said. "Now I have to get me a nap. Wake me at eleven, Annie."

"MOVE THE MOON," someone shouted. "Move the goddamn *moon*. The moon's gotta be over here, for God's sake."

Salter looked up at the night sky, but the voices were coming from behind a light as blinding as a searchlight, eighteen or twenty feet up, on a structure that Salter couldn't see behind the light. A second "moon," slightly less brilliant, was shining from a scaffold farther along the quay. There were, he counted, six other sources of light, each one attended by five or six people, all of whom seemed to be shouting.

As he approached the set, picking his way over the bundles of cables snaking across the quay, he tried to compose a simile to convey the scene to Annie when he got home. The equipment for the overhead shots—the cherry picker, the crane—and the scaffolding for the lamps combined into an image reminiscent of Cape Canaveral just before lift-off, but as he got closer and stepped to avoid the rails laid down for the camera, he was reminded of a movie he had seen about a group of resistance workers preparing to blow up a French train at a major junction. He hardly noticed anymore the ring of fifteen or sixteen Winnebagos.

All along the police barricades new sentries had been posted within sight of each other. Salter identified himself and picked his way over the bundles of cables snaking across the quay.

While Salter was watching the electricians, Ranovic appeared out of the darkness. "You read the end of this scene?" he asked. "Read it. It's a perfect setup."

"What are you talking about?"

"Read it. I'll wait around and we can talk."

There was plenty of time before the first shot, and Salter fetched his copy of the script from the glove compartment of his car.

There was no actual chase scene now. The script went from the house in Oakville straight to Vigor driving into the harbor parking lot, with Diamond close behind him.

The next scene began with Vigor arriving at Harbourfront and hurrying toward his boat. He is followed by Diamond, who had picked up the trail along the lakeshore. (His gamble has paid off.) Vigor is aware that Diamond is somewhere behind him, and he hurries to his boat and begins to untie it. He is balked by the second knot, and he takes out a knife and slashes at the mooring rope. At that point, a neighboring boat owner shouts at him to ask him what he is doing, and Vigor pulls out a gun and shoots him from about ten feet away. He cuts the boat free, starts the engine, and maneuvers the boat out of the mooring.

Diamond, in the meantime, is scrambling across the pedestrian bridge over the quay, and just as Vigor passes under the footbridge, he drops onto the back of the boat. In the final scene, Diamond and Vigor stalk each other around the boat, with Vigor taking potshots at his enemy, but Diamond manages to get below and open a valve to scuttle the boat. The movie ends with a struggle in the water interrupted by the Harbour Police. They pull Diamond from the lake, but Vigor has disappeared. They search for Vigor's body in ever-widening circles, and when they are far enough away from the nearly sunken boat to make an effective camera shot, Vigor is outlined on the prow, the only part still out of the water. He calls to Diamond, raises his gun, and one of the police shoots him; the police grapple his dead body from the lake. As they drag him aboard, his shirt opens, and we see an Iron Cross around his neck.

"So what's the problem?" Salter asked Ranovic.

"Don't you see! Those guns! They've already tried to get Diamond. All they have to do is put real bullets in Vigor's piece and they've got a perfect setup. Vigor can kill Diamond, and you'd have to figure out who switched the bullets.''

"This movie is getting to you, you know that? That and those Sunday evening television shows.''

That was Salter's first reaction to his certainty that Ranovic had just reinvented one of the hoariest chestnuts in crime fiction. His second reaction was to take it apart, bit by bit. "In the first place, *they* didn't try to get Diamond. That just happens in the movie. Diamond got into a scuffle with some kid. We don't know who he was, but he wasn't a professional. Secondly, Vigor almost certainly wouldn't hit Diamond when they are running around the boat. He's much more likely to hit the other boat owner, and what the hell's the point of killing some minor actor?''

"The *other boat owner*!'' Ranovic yelled. "Well, Jesus. Let's not have that happen. Talk to the props guy. He's in charge of guns.''

Salter sighed. "I'm going to look like a horse's ass, but all right. I'll make sure they're just pop guns.''

"Another thing. You know, when Vigor is aiming at Diamond in the last scene, just before the boat goes under? It wouldn't work. He's been in the lake, so the gun would be wet. There's no threat there.''

"Are we talking about the movie now?''

"Yeah.''

"This isn't a Civil War movie. I don't know if you have to keep your powder dry anymore, but my guess is they've invented a waterproof gun by now. Or maybe that's the point. The audience—people like you—know the gun won't fire, but the marine-unit cop kills him, anyway, because he's stupid. That's it. The subtext is really about how dumb the cops are.''

"You sure?"

"What do I know? But that's their script."

"You're the adviser. Shouldn't you tell them?"

Salter had seen this coming, a real "why-don't-you." "I tell you what," he said. "You tell 'em."

"Who should I speak to?"

"Fisher, the writer. He'll be very interested in your comments."

"He's not around anymore."

SALTER INSISTED TO himself that Ranovic's suggestion that someone might switch the bullets in Vigor's gun was ridiculous. Nevertheless, he mentioned it to Crabtree as lightly as he could. Crabtree didn't laugh, but led him over to the props man, and Salter repeated himself, feeling steadily more foolish.

The props man, Ben Quittenton, didn't laugh, either. He waited for Crabtree to go away, then took Salter over to his van. "As a matter of fact," he said, "the possibility crossed my mind. It always does, but this time I didn't flick it away." He unlocked the van. "Come in here. The reason it crossed my mind is that someone has been poking around my van. I don't know who, but when we were figuring out how to clean off the swastikas, I was looking for something, and I realized somebody had been turning my equipment over. Nothing was gone as far as I could tell—I have a lot of stuff here, and I don't have an inventory—and they certainly didn't touch the guns. I checked them." He took a key from his pocket and unlocked the lid of a counter. Underneath were a dozen guns, real and toy, including the pistol Vigor was to use. "See?" He took out the magazine. "It's empty. Now, here are the blanks." He pulled a small cardboard box from a drawer, still under its original factory seals, and broke it open. He pulled out a cartridge. "They haven't any heads," he pointed out. "They just make a noise."

"When do you load it?"

"Just before the scene is set."

"Then what do you do with it?"

"I give it to Henry Vigor last thing before he goes up in front of the cameras. I'll be setting him up with a holster beforehand."

"After you've loaded it, can you keep it on you?"

"I could." Quittenton weighed the gun in his hand. "Look, no one's listening. Let's be silly about this, shall we? This whole operation has got me goosey. Here . . . here's eight slugs. *You* keep 'em. When we're ready, I'll get you to load the gun."

"Yeah, well, I asked a silly question. This is the answer, I guess." He took the slugs from Quittenton and put them in an inside pocket.

"We won't tell a soul," Quittenton promised.

"You've no idea who could have been in here?"

"It could have been anyone. I leave it unlocked a lot of the time—not the guns—and people get curious. It looks like a museum. Fisher's been in here a few times, and the guy who drives the makeup truck. He's fascinated by it. I don't mind if they come around when I'm here, and I've never actually found anyone in the truck when I came back from being away, no."

Salter strolled back to the action and found Seth talking to Henry Vigor. Lately, the boy had been watching for every chance between his dance rehearsals to get away and watch the movie, but it was a surprise to find him getting back and forth on his own, especially after the day he had put in.

"How did you get down at this time of night?"

"Mom gave me a ride. You took off before I could catch you."

"How did you get past the guards?"

"I asked them where I could find you. I was just talking to Mr. Vigor about the end of the movie. Where is he going in his boat? I mean, does he always have it ready to make his getaway? Where to? Buffalo? They could just wait for him across the lake. I would."

Salter considered. "He's picked up by an amphibian plane in the middle of the lake. He radios for help from the boat."

"You're kidding, Dad."

"Of course I'm kidding. How do I know?"

Vigor said. "Seth is a realist. He's like the boy in the Hemingway story who can't understand why the naked sword between the two lovers would be a problem. Like that boy, Seth would roll right over it."

Seth blushed slightly. "Yeah, but this is supposed to be a realistic movie, isn't it? It's a thriller."

"No, no. I'll tell you the story. Once upon a time there was a wicked man who had done great wrong to the king's subjects, but when the king's guards went to find him, he had disappeared. They searched and searched, but they couldn't find him. Then one day a young man appeared at the court looking for the wicked man because he had done great wrong to his father, too. So the king gives him a purse of gold and tells him to look some more. A good wizard tells the young man that the wicked man lives nearby, disguised as a merchant. But a wicked wizard warns the merchant, and he gets away before the young man can capture him. The wicked man travels to the seashore because there he can sail away and the young man will never find him, but the young man gets a pair of magic boots from the good wizard and makes it to the shore ahead of the wicked man, tears off the wicked man's disguise, and the wicked man melts into the sea. It's a fairy story, Seth. Like a ballet. So the answer to your question 'Where is the wicked man going?' is not 'Buffalo' but 'Far away.' Realistically, the whole thing is a pile of tosh, but it's one of my favorite stories. I've played that wicked man a dozen times. I'm very fond of him.''

"See?" Salter said. He strolled back to the set and found Crabtree waiting for him.

"I just thought of something else," Salter said. "Doesn't Diamond take the Iron Cross from that house in Oakville? How come it's around Henry's neck in that last shot, just before he goes into the lake? When did Henry get it back?"

"Oh, for Christ's sake. Fisher was proud of that shot. BILL! Where the hell's Bill?" He walked off, bawling for the director.

Helena appeared carrying two plastic cups of coffee.

Salter said, "Henry's over by his trailer."

"I brought one of these for you. Nothing is happening. Let's go and sit by the lake."

She led him along the catwalk to the sea wall, handed him the two coffees, and made herself a perch on the wall, her legs dangling over the lake. Salter handed her the coffee, then joined her on the wall.

"Where did Seth go?" Salter asked.

"I passed him going to the commissary truck. He wanted to get a Coca-Cola so he could baby-sit Henry."

"Ah." Salter spread his arms along the top of the wall. Somewhere across the lake there were lights. Rochester? Buffalo?—he didn't know. It might as well be Calais or Monte Carlo. He breathed in deeply, catching her perfume and the faintest whiff of the camphor that seemed to accompany her, even when she was not carrying her enormous bag. "This is nice," he said.

"Helena," someone shouted. "Where the hell is Helena?"

They were getting ready to shoot the scene of Henry Vigor arriving. Salter picked his way through the chaos and found Vigor already established in a chair, drinking the brown liquid from his flask. He called Salter over and sent Sherriff for another chair.

"We found a beautiful canoe, did Seth tell you? He was very helpful."

"Good. I'm glad we're getting something back from those expensive camps we sent him to."

"I'm looking forward to Camilla's face when she sees it."

Sherriff came out of the darkness carrying a chair, which he thrust behind Salter's knees in a way to hurt a little.

"Let's go," Crabtree shouted.

"Thirty minutes, Henry," Sherriff said. "I'll come and get you."

Vigor turned to Salter. "Tell me about Harbourfront," he said. "What is it all about? Simon Ashley, the television writer, says he read from a novel here, so I know about the reading series. But what's the rest of it all about?"

Salter got a hint of what life must be like for Sherriff. The old man needed all kinds of attention, not the least of which was the simple company required to stave off boredom. This was the job he was assigning Salter when Sherriff was too busy.

Salter tried to explain the story of the rise and fall of Toronto's waterfront as a play space for the citizens of Toronto. "It was supposed to bring people downtown to the waterfront, but it brought developers instead. I don't understand what went wrong, but it isn't working as people say it should. It was supposed to be a playground for the people, but it's ending up like an exclusive section of Miami Beach. Next thing, you'll have the tenants of these places complaining to the police about undesirable elements hanging about. That'll be what's left of the people trying to get a look at the lake."

All the time he was talking to Vigor, Salter was conscious of the other reality, the scene in the movie that was slowly coming together under the lights. He was conscious, too, of the reality beyond the lights, of the guards waiting for the wrecker prowling the set, waiting for his next chance.

"Some people do use it, though," Vigor said. "Tom brought me down here last Sunday. It was packed with families having a day out. Do you know the most interesting thing? There were so many different kinds. The children, especially, look as if they've been brought together to pose for one of those pictures of children from many lands put out by UNICEF."

QUITTENTON, the props man, appeared and equipped Vigor with his holster. The actor practiced taking out the gun a few times, then Quittenton held out his hand to Salter for the blanks. Together they loaded the gun and handed it back to Vigor.

"What is this?" Vigor asked.

"Just a precaution, Henry."

"Dear God," Vigor said when he saw the implications of what they were doing. "Dear God. Perhaps I should be getting a guarantee that this thing is harmless."

"That's what we're giving you," Quittenton said. "Don't take it out until you use it. They're ready for you now."

It didn't take long to film Vigor getting out of the car, then to reposition the camera to shoot him from behind as he moved to his boat. Salter, watching, was reminded of Ranovic's admiration for Vigor. He, too, found it astonishing to see the transformation in the actor from gentle old man to hunted war criminal as soon as the cameras rolled, the sense of ruthlessness he conveyed, as if he had been injected with villainy, and the transformation back to old gentleman as soon as the scene was over.

"It's called acting," Quittenton said quietly in his ear. "Did you see your wife, by the way? She was looking for you."

"My wife? When?"

"About half an hour ago. She brought your boy down and wanted to talk to me about props, but I'm kinda busy, so she went off and looked for you. Someone said they'd seen you over by the lake. She find you?"

Salter ignored the question. "Then what? Did she go home?"

"I guess, if she couldn't find you."

NOW THE CAMERAS were set for the shot of Vigor untying the ropes. This scene would be cut into by a shot of the neighboring boat owner appearing; then the camera would return to Vigor, taking out his gun and firing. The final shot would be of the boat owner looking at his chest in surprise, then slumping to the deck. Vigor scuttled along the wharf and started to untie the knots, then took out his knife and slashed the rope free. As he did so, there was a shout from the darkness, and Vigor looked up, pulled out his gun, and fired. He finished slashing the rope, stepped aboard, and started the engine. In spite of all his precautions, Salter was relieved when there was no scream from the darkness.

When Vigor's part was complete, the camera was repositioned on the deck of Vigor's boat, and the lights were directed on the neighboring yacht. A figure emerged, shouted, "Hey," jerked backward as Vigor shot him, grabbed his chest, and slid slowly downward as a thin trickle of blood escaped from the corner of his mouth.

Salter said, "What the hell?"

Connors shouted, "Cut," and Ranovic got to his feet, grinning. Connors said, "Dammit, who put that blood capsule in his mouth?"

Ranovic said, "That was my idea." To Salter, he said, "Now you know why I wanted to be sure that second boat owner was safe."

Connors said, "Then we'll have to do it again, without the blood. There's no blood called for, d'ye see? You're shot in the chest. There'd be no blood for a few minutes, d'ye see? So leave the goddamn blood *out*, d'ye hear?" The normally mild-mannered Connors was having trouble finding an adequate vocabulary to express his fury. Ranovic shrugged, wiped his mouth, winked at Salter, and disappeared to start the scene again.

Crabtree said to Salter, "He's been bugging me to let him into a scene since we started. This was an emergency. I decided, under the circumstances, the scene could be dangerous and the proper man to get shot would be a cop."

"What about ACTRA?" was all Salter could think of to say. The appearance of Ranovic had upset him. When Ranovic had appeared instead of the minor actor he had been expecting, the frame of artifice had been broken so that Ranovic's apparent slaughter had seemed to be outside the film, to be real.

"That's what I'm saying. Fuck ACTRA. They've already listed seven complaints against me. I'm trying to prevent one of their members from being killed."

"What was the emergency?"

"Fisher. He was supposed to do the scene. He thinks he's Hitchcock, and he always writes in a little part for himself. I forgot I'd banned him from the set. I thought of your guy instead. I must've been feeling cute, because I think I'm going to be able to finish the picture, Charlie."

"Even with Ranovic farting around?"

Crabtree smiled. They watched Ranovic act for a few more takes; then Connors called a halt, and they set up for the scene of Vigor's boat maneuvering out of the mooring.

"How did I do?" Ranovic wanted to know. "Did it look right?"

"You did fine."

"I didn't know how to play it. I thought maybe I should kind of spin around, but that always looks phony to me. I had to look inside me to find something I had really experienced, you know? Then I remembered that television shot of Harvey Oswald."

"You did fine. Go on the stage. Get yourself a union card."

"You remember he kind of doubled forward?"

"For Christ's sake, Ranovic. Ask Crabtree for a print of the scene. Then you can put it in your portfolio for your next audition."

But Ranovic was not to be denied. "The thing is, you have to really *think* what it must be like. You see this guy cutting the rope, and there you are, normal law-abiding civilian, and then, pow, something hits you in the guts."

"In the chest."

"What?"

"In your case, you got shot in the chest. Don't confuse yourself with Oswald."

But Ranovic wasn't listening anymore. Seeing the look on his face, Salter was reminded of the joke about the man who looked after the elephants at the circus, and he hoped that Ranovic was only temporarily infected by show business. But it looked bad.

Two hours later, as the first hint of light appeared in the east, Diamond scrambled aboard Vigor's boat for the last time, and Sherriff pronounced it a wrap.

"I was just thinking," Crabtree said. "Wouldn't it have been beautiful if Fisher had played the part and Ranovic had been right and the gun had really been loaded and you hadn't told me? Too bad I warned him to stay off the set."

WHAT WAS LEFT of Sunday should have been a day of rest, but Salter woke at noon to a cool, offhand Annie doing laundry, gardening, and driving off in the car without telling him where she was going.

When she returned, he asked her twice what was wrong and got the reply "Nothing." He had to wait until they were in bed, when he asked her for the last time, and she turned away from him as she said, "Does she have pretty underwear?"

"For God's sake," Salter protested, and made several attempts to get her into an argument, but Annie preferred to nurse her certainty in silence until finally Salter decided the hell with it and went to sleep.

AT EIGHT O'CLOCK on Monday morning a squad car appeared outside Salter's door, and Salter went to the door for the message.

"Staff Inspector Salter?" The constable looked impressed with the importance of his message. "I've been sent to fetch you, sir. There's been a homicide, and they think you ought to be there."

"Who?"

"They didn't say, sir. Just a homicide."

PART THREE

THIRTEEN

As Salter arrived at the front door of the Argylle Hotel, a fireman came out carrying an oxygen cylinder. Salter showed his identification. "He still alive?"

"Not this one." The fireman hoisted the cylinder onto his shoulder and moved off to his emergency truck.

Two ambulance attendants appeared, one of them carrying a rolled-up stretcher.

"See you later?" the constable guarding the door asked.

"Not us. We only handle emergencies. Life-threatening ones."

Salter showed his card to the constable.

"Elevator to the second floor, sir, then straight along the corridor. Don't use the stairs."

Inside, another policeman was guarding the route to the victim's room. Salter understood what was happening: The police were trying to keep the immediate area as uncontaminated as possible. When he got off the elevator, there was another constable waiting to direct him along the corridor. On every floor now there would be an officer directing traffic along a single path, keeping people away from the stairs.

As he reached the room, a plainclothes policeman came out. Salter recognized him as a member of the Homicide squad, though he had never met him.

"Staff Inspector Salter? I'm Sergeant Burnley."

Salter nodded and moved toward the door of the bedroom.

"Could you hold on for a minute? There's still some work to do."

Through the doorway Salter could see three or four technicians working around the body. When a victim of a violent assault is discovered, the first job is to preserve life. Thus, the fire department and the ambulance team are called. After them, and in spite of them, the police must also try to preserve the scene intact. The more people who contaminate the scene, including the medics, the harder it is to isolate the evidence. In this case, Salter guessed that the emergency crews had been able to do their job almost without touching the body. Fisher lay on his back, naked except for his boxer shorts, an old military dagger sticking out of his chest.

"Let's go down to the lobby," Burnley said. "There's a pot of coffee there for us." It was eight o'clock.

THE LOBBY WAS EMPTY except for two American couples who had formed a group in one corner to watch the excitement. Burnley took Salter to some armchairs near the window and signaled to the constable that they wanted to be left alone. Salter waited while the sergeant fetched them some coffee. Burnley returned, took out a pack of cigarettes, got Salter's permission, and lit up.

"The coroner been?" Salter asked.

Burnley nodded. "Robinson, thank Christ. You know him?"

"I don't know any of them."

"Robinson's all right. Doesn't fart around playing Sherlock Holmes like Juba. Just does his job and leaves us to ours."

"What did he say?"

"He thinks it may be an amateur. We'll wait for the autopsy, of course, but the guy was stabbed a lot of times, as if the killer was trying to make sure, although there isn't much blood and the victim never moved after the first wound, which probably was the fatal one. He almost looks as if he was stabbed in his sleep."

"Could the coroner tell anything about the killer?"

"He says if the killer was on the left side of the bed, he was right-handed, but if he was on the right, he was probably left-handed." Burnley smiled slightly. "Robinson's a comedian. So what can you tell me?"

"How did you find out about me?"

"The usual way, the duty desk."

"I don't know the routine."

Burnley spread his fingers and began ticking points off. "The desk clerk at the hotel made the first call." He looked up inquisitively to see if Salter understood him thus far.

Salter nodded.

"Fisher had a regular wake-up call in for six-thirty. He used to jog. When the desk clerk didn't get any reply, he went up to Fisher's room and knocked on the door. Then he got concerned. He knew Fisher'd come home the night before and hadn't left his key at the desk early this morning, didn't go jogging or anything like that, so the clerk used his own key to take a look. Found him like he is now. He called 911, and our guys turned up." Burnley had reached his thumb. "They called the emergency people and also the duty inspector at headquarters. The duty inspector called us out, and we took a look and posted the scene to wait for the technicians. Half an hour ago, when we phoned in Fisher's ID, someone told us about you.''

''Where are you now?''

''They've nearly finished the room; then they have to do the stairs and doorways. We're knocking on doors. After that we'll do the area. Next of kin are being informed, but they're in California someplace. You can do the identification for us. What's the story? He's some kind of writer on the movie you're investigating, right?''

''He's the scriptwriter.''

They were interrupted by the desk clerk, who was waving a telephone from across the room. Burnley took the call and returned to his chair. ''They've finished the room. They're doing the fire escape now. But tell me what you know first, before we go up there.''

Sergeant Burnley was a very experienced investigator. He had just given a little verbal demonstration to a staff inspector that he knew what he was doing, and now he wanted information, because it was his case, not Salter's. Now, as far as he was concerned, Salter was merely a useful witness.

Salter began slowly, stumbling at first. He had to tell the whole story of the sabotage, the rivalries, the quarrels, as succinctly as he could, but leaving nothing out. Gradually, he became more fluent as he left the elementary facts behind and got to the people Burnley would be concerned about.

Burnley listened patiently, taking no notes, but when Salter seemed to be finished, he pulled out his notebook and a ballpoint pen. ''Right. Now let's have it all again.''

"All of it?"

"Go through the whole thing so I understand it."

This time Burnley interrupted at every name. "Crabtree, the producer guy. He was on the outs with Fisher?"

"The other way around, I'd say."

Burnley made a note.

"This guy Sherriff. He get into a fight with Fisher?"

"Not as far as I know."

"The two big actors?"

"You can forget about Henry Vigor. He's over eighty years old. But Paul Diamond and Fisher didn't like each other, or rather, as with Crabtree, Fisher didn't like Diamond."

"You think Fisher could've been behind assaulting Diamond? Sorry. That's your investigation. You'd've covered that. But we could overlap."

"It looks that way. How will we work it?"

Burnley shook his head. "No, sir, we won't. I'll investigate the homicide, using your investigation as a source of suspects. If you get anywhere with your investigation, which from what you tell me isn't likely, it may throw something up for me. Otherwise, we'll go our way, you go yours, unless the deputy interferes. What about this Banjani woman? The coroner says amateur. Could've been a woman."

"I don't know of any connection between her and Fisher."

"But Crabtree might. He figured a connection, I mean."

Salter shrugged.

Burnley put down his notebook. "We've got two separate investigations, but at some point I might have to question everyone on the set. How many?"

"Fifty, maybe seventy-five."

"Jesus Christ. Let's go up to the room. Before I heard about you, I had my own ideas, which are a hell of a lot simpler than this can of worms you've been telling me about."

Burnley's colleague was waiting for them in Fisher's room.

"You know Sergeant Doig? This is Staff Inspector Salter."

Doig grunted and shook hands in perfunctory fashion, treating Salter as a rival, a Mountie, even. Not a member of the homicide squad, anyway.

Salter and Burnley moved over to look at Fisher's body. Burnley said, "I'm hoping the autopsy will simplify things for us. See how peaceful he is? No struggle, nothing. It looks to us like a sex killing."

"A whore?"

"Maybe, but whores don't make their living killing their customers. We found his wallet, and we found a packet of condoms in the bathroom, so he had it in mind to have a little fun while he was here. What we need to know from the pathologist is if there is any semen around."

Salter waited.

From the window, Doig, still keeping his distance from Salter, said, "His or anyone else's."

Salter, lacking their experience, was puzzled. "Anyone else's?"

"That's right," Doig continued. "As Sergeant Burnley says, whores don't stab their customers un-less—but there's no liquor around. Ballet boys do, though."

Salter turned around to look at Doig now. "And what's a ballet boy?"

"A kid. A chicken. A male prostitute."

"Why ballet boy? That your own name for them?"

Burnley interrupted. "It's just a name." He turned again to look at the body. "You see how simple that would make it for us? If there was two kinds of semen, then we'd know what we're dealing with." He adopted a friendly tone to cut off the odd hostility that had sprung up between Salter and Doig, who could be a surly bastard sometimes.

"SO," SALTER SAID after a pause, "that'll tell you what you're looking for, will it? What then?"

"Then we look around the track, Wellesley Street mainly, show Fisher's picture around, see if anyone remembers him cruising."

"That'll simplify things, all right. But I'll tell you this now: I'll be very surprised if Fisher was anything but straight."

"People usually are surprised. But chicken hawks come in every shape—judges, lawyers, stockbrokers."

"No cops?"

"Haven't come across one yet. But cops don't get to travel much. Some of these guys only feel safe out of town."

Salter's paranoia subsided under the influence of Burnley's matter-of-fact tone, and he realized that all he was hearing was a homicide sergeant quoting his experience, not speaking out of his prejudices.

"Why would a male prostitute kill his client any more than a hooker would?"

"Some of them aren't very stable, the shrinks have told us. They don't like what they're doing, and they blame the client. If they get too disgusted, they crack up. Especially if they're on drugs, like most of them.''

"Uh-huh." Salter looked around the room. It was even barer than most hotel rooms, because Fisher's clothes and anything loose that might have been touched had already been taken to the lab. "You find any drugs?" he asked.

"Nope. Just the packet of condoms. Otherwise, just his clothes, a couple of books, and his shaving stuff.''

"Well, lotsa luck. You know where to find me.''

Burnley was looking through some charge slips. "I took these out of his wallet before we sent it to the lab. You any idea who Fisher used to eat dinner with? I'll have to check up on these.''

Salter took the slips. There were five of them, two from restaurants Salter knew and three he had heard of. "No. You want me to look after them?''

Automatically, Burnley reached for the slips, shaking his head. Then he stopped. "Yeah.'' He looked at Doig. "He knows these people. We could get a description that wouldn't mean anything to us.''

Doig shrugged and turned away.

"Check them out for us," Burnley said to Salter. "If you've got the time.''

Salter put the receipts in his wallet. "I'll be in touch when I've been the rounds.''

"We'll see you before then. If we do overlap, then you're going to have to be there when we question the crew.''

"Whatever you say. Now, do I know everything you know yet?''

"Let me look after this first." Burnley picked up the phone and made arrangements for Fisher's body to be taken away, then turned back to Salter. "No one saw

him come home last night," he began. "But around
ten o'clock he asked the desk for a message. There
weren't any. No one came in after that looking for
him. The room next door was unoccupied. No one saw
or heard anything unusual. He'd never brought any
women up to the room that the desk clerk knew of. He
said the guy had no visitors and hardly any phone
calls. He called Los Angeles every night, his answering service, and twice he got collect calls from a
woman down there. That's it. They've got his Visa
number at the desk. Nobody else from L.A. was staying here. There was no one hanging around the lobby
last night."

"What about the fire escape?"

There was a sound from Doig like a small hiss of
disgust.

"We found a palm print on the inside of the door.
I'm guessing it's Fisher's. The room is full of prints,
though they couldn't get any off the knife. It's got a
rope handle. What we need is a suspect."

"Where do you look when a stranger from out of
town gets stabbed in his hotel room?"

"When he's in his shorts, we look for reasons in his
lifestyle, like I said."

"Apart from a sex act, I mean."

"It hasn't happened to me yet. How about you,
Howard?"

"Once," Doig said. "That was a drug problem.
Guy came up from Detroit to collect his money, and
that's how he got paid. Sooner or later some scum will
tip us a word, but until then we're not busting our
asses on it. Let 'em kill each other off. But I've never
had an innocent guy hurt. You'll have to find a story."

"IT'S GOT TO BE connected," Salter said.

They were in his office that afternoon. Orliff had dropped by on a visit to town and had heard about Fisher's death.

"You think Fisher found out something?"

"If he did, I need to know who he's seen in the last couple of days. He's been banned from the set for three days," Salter said. "Maybe someone found out about Fisher."

"Found out what? Why would Fisher be wrecking the film?"

"Spite. He had a real mean streak."

"Would he go that far?"

"No," Salter confessed. "When Diamond was mugged, Fisher did a good rewrite job to keep the film going. And he had some of his own money in it."

"What line is Burnley taking?"

Salter told him of the Doig theory of a male prostitute.

"I wouldn't have thought so. But I wouldn't get in Burnley's way, just in case he comes up with something. Killing Fisher doesn't hurt the movie, does it?"

"Not as far as I can see. His job was over. I met this guarantor you talked about last week. Very impressive character. He'd've finished the film, no matter what."

"How?" Orliff was intrigued. "How would they have brought off the chase scene at the end? Without Diamond, say."

Salter took a mouthful of coffee. "Long shots, look-alikes," he said authoritatively. "At the end, you have a pal of Diamond's, in the film, I mean, telling us how he killed Vigor after he saw Vigor kill his friend Diamond."

"Oh, very good, Charlie. Not too exciting, though. The only connection I can see is that Fisher wrote the film and someone could be out to get the film and its author. An anti-Semite."

Salter said, "Someone like that would surely know which way around a swastika went."

"Did you find the guy who hit Diamond yet?"

"No, and I watched Diamond fight the other day. I think he would have hit him pretty hard."

"Where have you looked?"

"We checked all the Metro hospitals." Salter was moving around the office now. "I'd better be getting back."

"Maybe you should go beyond Metro. I know you didn't want to raise the country for a little assault case, Charlie, but this is homicide now."

"Maybe I should just leave it to the experts." Salter had opened the door and was looking around the room to see if he had forgotten anything.

"I wouldn't do that yet. Like I said, don't get in Burnley's way, but do your job. If they find the killer, they're liable to solve your other case. And if they don't, it won't be their fault, because you were in charge at the crucial time."

That was what Orliff came to tell him, a useful reminder from an old politician who had always survived. Salter stopped bustling and gave Orliff his attention again. "I also want to talk to the people who know Fisher at home," he said. "Just in case they know of some vendetta, or anything Fisher was mixed up in, that spilled over up here."

"I can help you there. That guy I told you about, the scriptwriter I'm taking fishing, he's in Montreal. He called me. He's coming to town in the next day or so, if that's soon enough. I'll ask him to set aside some time for you."

"Great."

Finally, Orliff stood up. "Keep me posted. Come up to the cottage soon. I've got half the siding on now." He looked around Salter's office. "I'm very objective these days, Charlie. See, I don't give a fuck."

Yes, you do, Salter thought. Not much of a fuck, but you are trying to look after me. All right. For the moment, anyway.

Orliff left the office, and Salter asked the computer people to put his request on the screens across the country. Did any emergency ward report an assault case on the night Diamond was attacked, probably involving a broken cheekbone? If the response was negative, he would try New York State and Michigan.

He got a response within two hours. A hospital in St. Catherines had reported exactly the kind of injury he described to the Niagara police. They had interviewed the man, who claimed to have been assaulted by someone who came out from under a bridge near the radio station, which was possible. Where was he now? They didn't know, but they could supply his name and social security number. Jaroslav Hasek, 413-876-707.

Salter asked for a check on the number and found it didn't exist, the name appeared on no computer listing. He telephoned the hospital and managed to get hold of the doctor on duty that night. He remembered the incident and could give Salter a description. Young, maybe twenty-two, fair-haired, Czech.

"Czech?"

"That's right. He didn't speak a lot of English, but we tried everything, and that's what it turned out he was. A pleasant kid, not the type to get mixed up in fights, except maybe playing hockey."

SALTER PUT THE PHONE DOWN, feeling unnerved that Orliff's suggestion had paid off so quickly, and, perhaps, significantly. But he knew his next move. It was time to call Ottawa. It was just possible that he had lifted a corner of a rug too big for him to handle.

Gudgeon was very friendly, pleased that Salter was taking him seriously, and agreed to find out if any of his connections had ever heard of Jaroslav Hasek. "For a simple homicide inquiry, we could ask the embassy in Prague. They're closed now, it's nighttime, but I'll find out and get back to you tomorrow afternoon."

SALTER STILL HOPED that Fisher had simply been unlucky in his choice of sex partners, but the next morning, Burnley came through with the news that the pathologist's report indicated that no sexual activity of any kind had taken place before the stabbing. In return, Salter reported the result of his renewed investigation of Diamond's assault and his conversation with Gudgeon.

"Christ," Burnley said. "It sounds like an international conspiracy. I'll take a good old-fashioned fag bashing anytime. Let's go and talk to these movie people."

FOURTEEN

BEFORE THEY COULD get started with the interviewing, Quittenton, the props man, asked to see him.

"I understand that Fisher was stabbed and you've got the knife," Quittenton said.

Salter nodded and waited, guessing what was coming.

"A dagger, maybe? With a rope handle?"

"Something like that. It looked like army issue."

"I think it belonged to me. You remember I told you while we were worrying about the gun that someone had been in my van. I heard about the dagger on the grapevine, so I checked. Mine is missing."

"I'll have them show it to you."

He reported back to Burnley.

"I guess we overlap, after all," Burnley said.

"Unless Fisher swiped the knife himself and the killer just grabbed whatever was handy."

INTERVIEWING THE FILM CREW was a tedious business. Crabtree loaned them his office in the warehouse/studio, and they disposed quickly of most of the crew, asking only for some proof of their whereabouts on the night Fisher was killed. Salter was aware that Burnley was keeping a steady eye out for any males who might have known Fisher well enough to visit him via the fire escape, but the homicide detective found no one to solve his case so easily.

They began their interviews of the major figures with Crabtree himself. Salter opened with a prepared speech about wanting to know if anyone on the set had any idea of Fisher's plans for Sunday night, but Crabtree quickly moved him on.

"I was with Carole Banjani on Sunday night," he said. "We had something to eat at the Swiss Chalet, then I took her home, and we stayed there until it was time to come down to Harbourfront."

Salter nodded. "Thanks for telling us. We have to check up on everybody now."

"I know that."

"Anything else we ought to know about you, Jack?"

Now Crabtree shrugged, and Salter thanked him again, dismissing him.

Carole Banjani repeated Crabtree's story. They asked her a few questions about times and let her go. On the whole, Salter said, he was inclined to believe her and Crabtree, though he kept an open mind. The alibis of two lovers had to be suspect, but until he found out anything to make him doubt their story, they could not come down on them too hard.

Sherriff was next, and he simply offered the information that he had spent the evening in a bar on Bloor Street. He named several people who had seen him there, although the actual times were vague. He did not much seem to care that his movements were not closely verifiable. Once more, they decided to leave it there for the moment.

"You don't have any idea where Fisher was that night?" Burnley asked.

"Nope."

"Or if he was with anyone?"

"Nope."

"Thanks." Burnley tried to create the impression of a man who has satisfactorily cleared up a detail.

They talked to Connor, to Hodek, through him to the cameraman, Tessier, and to half a dozen others, including Helena, but no one had anything to offer. Before they let Helena go, Salter took the opportunity to cross another item off his list, asking her if she could remember anything about the incident of the sprinklers. Terry Dresden, the publicity photographer, had supplied him with half a dozen pictures of the scene that he had taken in case they had some comic publicity value. In all of them the actors and the crew were looking wet and astonished, and in two of them Helena's camphor-laden bag could be seen tucked under a chair.

"Where was Fisher when the sprinkler started to rain?" Salter asked.

"I don't know. Why?"

"Because he isn't in any of the pictures and he never missed a scene while I was around. Do you remember seeing him hanging about, offstage? Off camera?"

She took the pictures off him and stared at them. "You saw my bag," she said. "Of course. No, I can't be sure. I don't remember seeing him, and that would be the only kind of scene he might not want to watch, because it is just of Paul and his wife in the movie. But I don't remember not seeing him, either. Everyone was making such a fuss."

Salter nodded. "I'll ask the others," he said.

When she had gone, he said to Burnley, "Just for a minute there I thought Fisher was my answer. Be nice to be sure of something." Finally, Salter managed to have a word with Ranovic and told him to spread the word, especially to Crabtree, that Burnley was operating on the assumption that Fisher was killed by a prostitute.

Late in the day they went back to the office, where Burnley showed Salter the pathologist's report. There were a number of wounds, none very deep, and in the pathologist's opinion the killer was not very strong, perhaps old or a woman. And there was no semen of any kind, the lab reported.

The fingerprint people confirmed Burnley's guess that the palm print on the fire door was Fisher's.

"So Fisher let someone in, he was probably looking for sex, but he got killed looking. So anything is possible, not excluding prostitutes, male and female. Jesus. This is starting to look *difficult*," Burnley said.

They had some routine procedures in each investigation, and the next move in the investigation of Fisher's death was to check up on the charge slips that they had found in Fisher's wallet; but before Salter could do that, Bernard Simple, Orliff's scriptwriter-contact and Fisher's friend in Hollywood, appeared at his office.

A thin face, bright with intelligence when he talked but continually fading into abstractedness while he was listening, as if he had understood the message from the first three words and was working on another problem while he waited for Salter to finish the sentence. Salter guessed he was in his forties: a California tan, perfect teeth, and a high, polished, bald cranium, but with plenty of well-barbered black hair on the back and sides.

"You've heard my problem?" Salter asked.

"Someone killed Stan Fisher."

"You don't sound surprised."

"I've accepted it by now. Orliff told me yesterday. Sure, I'm surprised. Stan wasn't the world's nicest guy, on the surface, but he wasn't bad. It's just that for an intelligent man, I mean, a writer, he was incredibly stupid."

"How?"

"He was always offending people, and he used to take what he wanted without saying thanks."

Salter waited for amplification.

"I mean, if you made a witty remark to him over lunch, he'd be on a talk show the next day using it as if it were his. He was the kind of guy I would never tell an idea to."

"Could someone have killed him for stealing an idea? This movie, for instance?"

"Oh, no. There's nothing original about this movie except that it's set in Canada. Stan probably thought there was, but no one would chase him for stealing it."

"Was he a good writer?"

Simple laughed. "You saw the script. What do you think?"

"What do I know about writing?"

"As much as any producer, I guess. Look, that question is unanswerable in terms of screenplays. You don't write them. You put them together, you manufacture them. So he put together some screenplays that made the producers money, yes. He wasn't a bad novelist, though. Maybe that's the best answer I can give you. Yes, he was a pretty good thriller writer, and he thought he was raising the form to a species of literature. We all do. I write good thrillers myself, better than Fisher's." He laughed to take the conceit out of the remark, leaving it as a statement of fact.

"You were close to him?"

"I liked the guy, up to a point. We used to have lunch together quite often when we were both in town. We didn't talk about writing, though."

"Did you ever talk about anything that would interest me?"

Simple now looked bored stiff. "I don't know anyone or anything that might have been behind this. He had some money, he had a nice new girlfriend, what else?"

Salter was hoping not to have to say it because he knew how easy it was to suggest something, even to someone as apparently intelligent as Simple was, and have them pick it up and present it as a possibility. All conversations of this kind bordered on interrogation, and the interrogated one instinctively tried to respond with what the questioner wanted to hear. Nevertheless, he wanted to know something more. "Did he say anything about getting into trouble in Czechoslovakia?" he asked.

"He went there for the State Department or some such organization, didn't he?"

"That's right. Did he say anything?"

Simple was interested now. "You think he might have upset someone there?"

"I don't know. I'm just sorting out the chaff."

"Let's see. What did he tell me about that? First of all, he went to Europe a bit of a socialist and came back completely turned around. I think that was a pretty traumatic experience for an old sixties' rebel, which he said he was, though I don't remember seeing him there when I was protesting. He came back pretty spaced out about the amount of surveillance he was subjected to. He was naive, you know? Very anti-CIA and Reagan and all that, but never thinking twice about what it would be like to live in a place where everybody is informing on everyone else and you have to apply for permission to go on holiday.'' Again, Simple laughed. ''I think the thing that really pissed him off was that he was quite proud of having his books published behind the curtain until one of the publishers there told him they found his books inoffensive, like Agatha Christie's. That didn't please him at all.''

''But he never got into trouble with the authorities?''

''Not that he told me. He soon got over his paranoia, too, because when he came back, he wrote an article about life behind the curtain that was published in one of the local papers. I remember that because he used some lines I gave him. It was pretty mild stuff, though, which is why he couldn't get it published in New York or in a national magazine. He'd made the classic mistake of thinking that because it was such a learning experience for him, everyone would be interested, but it didn't amount to much. He found out the interpreters are often spies and the newspapers are censored—not a very big deal except when you actually experience it. I had the same thing happen in Moscow a couple of years before. If you think about it, you know it already, but you don't know it really until you've experienced it. Make sense?''

Salter nodded. ''This article? Where would I find it?''

Simple thought for a moment, then asked, ''You guys got a fax machine?''

''Sure. Hold on.'' Salter looked down a list taped to his desk. ''Here's the number.''

"Use your phone?"

Salter pushed it across the desk. Simple dialed a number with long-distance digits and was soon talking to someone in Los Angeles. "Honey," he said after a few courtesies, "call up Leonora at the paper, will you? About a year ago, in the Sunday supplement, there was an article by Stan Fisher. There was something about a curtain in the title. Ask her to fax a copy to this number, will you? It's a police inquiry. Staff Inspector Salter of the Toronto police. No, Canada. Thanks. I'll be home soon.

"You should have it this afternoon," he said to Salter. "I review books for the paper," he added by way of an explanation for his ability to provide the service. "How else can I help you? Just obvious stuff. He wasn't gay, he wasn't into drugs, he didn't take a woman off anyone lately, he was tight with his money, but I don't think he would cheat anyone. He was pushy and egotistical, like everyone else in L.A. And now I have to go."

"You've saved me a lot of trouble, Mr. Simple. Thanks."

"Yeah. You got a card? I might need a favor myself sometime. I collect these things, especially from cops." Simple offered a wide-splayed hand that Salter had to fold in order to shake, and left.

FIFTEEN

BURNLEY SAID, "There's someone waiting to see me, a cabdriver. Stay here while I talk to him."

The cabdriver was West Indian. "You are seeking information about a suspicious happening near the hotel on the night that man was killed?" he asked. He had a very neat and old-fashioned appearance: dark gray pants surmounted by a gleaming white shirt and a black tie.

"Did you see anyone around the back of the hotel, in the alley or on the fire escape?" Burnley asked.

"Not that, but four or five times I saw a man waiting nearby in the front, watching the hotel."

"Standing on the sidewalk? What did he look like?"

"He was in a car. A red Buick. License number YRM 248."

Salter blinked. "What made you take note of him?"

"He was in my parking space. There's room there for one cab, and I use it a lot. There's a good streetlight, and I like to study between trips. Every time I came back there from nine until about ten, he was there. Then, when I came back from a trip at about half past ten, he was gone, so I could get my space."

"Did you get a look at him?"

"Yes, I was going to talk to him, to tell him that there was no good waiting for prostitutes there. Tell him to go home to his wife."

"What did he look like?"

"A bad man." The cabdriver gave a detailed description.

"Thank you, Mr.?"

"Johnson."

"Thank you. By the way, what are you studying?"

Johnson looked at Salter for some time, seeming to be judging whether he could trust Salter with the information. "The Gospel," he said.

"I see. Thank you."

"That's what we need," Salter said. "A fleet of cabdrivers studying the Gospel, watching out for sin."

"Did you recognize the guy from the description?"

"Oh, yes. It was Sherriff, the assistant director."

"Let's go talk to him."

ON THE WAY OUT to Oakville, Burnley said, "How come we never worked together before?"

"I never worked Homicide."

"You've been involved in a couple of cases, though. I was talking to someone who mentioned that."

"Only by accident."

"What's the name of your unit again?"

Salter told him. Special Affairs.

Burnley made the obvious joke, then, "You solved the Yorkville bomb case, right?"

"We knew who it had to be from the start. The problem was figuring how he did it."

They dropped down off the Queen Elizabeth Way onto the Oakville road. "You must be getting ready to retire," Burnley said.

"Do I look that old? It's a bad light in here."

"No, but, you know. Your kids all through school?"

Salter understood now how much Burnley had been asking around about him. "No."

"How many do you have?"

"I've got two boys." Salter looked out at the highway to cut off the conversation.

"Both at college?"

Salter looked at the scenery for a few moments, then turned to look at Burnley. "One of them, the older one, is at Western, studying business. The other one is studying to be a dancer. A ballet boy, you might say, but not one of the kind you people deal with." He wished he hadn't added that. Screw Burnley. And it wasn't fair, either, and he had to admire Burnley for accepting it as if it were. Burnley just looked quizzical, nodded, and said nothing.

SHERRIFF SAID, "Okay, sure, I was waiting outside the hotel for an hour on Sunday night."

"For Fisher."

"For Fisher. I wanted to have a word with him."

"What about?"

"He'd been bad-mouthing me with Crabtree."

"Did you speak to him?"

"For a minute. In the street. I'm in enough trouble with Jack, so I told Fisher to keep his mouth shut. I never went inside the hotel."

"What time was this?"

"Around ten. Here. I've found a bar slip from where I went afterward. Timed and dated. These computer cash registers are useful." He smiled briefly.

"Why did we have to wait to find this out?"

Sherriff didn't bother to answer.

Burnley said, "It might have speeded me along."

"It might have speeded me into jail."

"It still might. Interfering with a police investigation. You don't have any more information for me? While you were waiting, did you see anyone else hanging around?"

"Like Jack Crabtree, maybe?" Sherriff barked with laughter. "No. No one."

"Was anyone with Fisher?"

"He came home by himself."

"All right. Go away. Not too far, though."

"IT FIGURES," Burnley said. "We'll check it with Crabtree, but I don't see Fisher letting Sherriff up the back stairs, do you? We needn't look for anyone Fisher was with that night. We need someone he didn't want to be seen with. A prostitute, maybe."

Burnley was seeking the easy answer, and Salter let him have it, for now.

CRABTREE CONFIRMED Sherriff's account. "Sherriff wanted a day off," he said. "Seems he felt he had one coming for driving Henry all over northern Ontario looking for a canoe. So he got one of the other A.D.s to cover for him and called in sick, but Fisher saw him having lunch at the Senator with some woman, and he told me."

"NOW WHAT?" Burnley asked.

"Now I go back to work, looking for the set wrecker."

"Don't you think you've found him?"

"Who?"

"Fisher. It's been obvious to me ever since you mentioned it that Fisher's your boy. For a while I figured that was why Fisher got killed. Now I figure there's no connection. Your guy, Fisher, was just naturally vicious.'' He smiled as at a private joke. ''Your job's done. My guy is someone who's never been near that movie.''

"SOMETHING COME FROM Los Angeles on the fax for you, sir.'' A civilian clerk walked in and dropped two sheets of paper on Salter's desk.

''Let me read this,'' Salter said to Ranovic. ''We are in the studio tomorrow. Right?''

''Right. Nine a.m.''

Salter nodded, already reading. ''I'll come and find you.''

The article was called ''Crime Behind the Curtain.'' Three months before the article appeared, Fisher had been invited on a speaking tour of several countries in the Eastern bloc where his novels were published: Romania, Hungary, and Czechoslovakia. Some part of the article dealt with how popular Fisher was behind the curtain. None of it seemed to point to an Eric Amblerish conspiracy. The last half of the article, however, seemed just possibly to have created offense in Czechoslovakia, where Fisher ended his tour. He had been provided with a guide, and Fisher had the usual things to say about the way in which all such people really worked for the secret police, although they didn't fool Fisher, but this time he had made a breakthrough. On the last day, he and the interpreter had found themselves with a lot of time on their hands, and they had spent the evening in a beer hall. The interpreter had drunk enough to relax and trust Fisher. He had told him all his hopes and dreams and about his forthcoming marriage, and he had poured out his dislike of the regime he was serving, how much he was longing for *glasnost* to come to Czechoslovakia, and a detailed account of the continual surveillance, distortion, censorship, and general misery that was his lot under the current regime.

Salter remembered Fisher talking about the experience. He had written it all, and it made lively reading. It might just be enough, Salter thought, at sea in the area of East/West propaganda games, to cause a government to want to pay back Fisher. It might even be personal: Fisher had been a guest, his way paid by the regime he was exposing. The object of Fisher's trip had surely been to make a friendly gesture, a demonstration by Czechoslovakia that it wanted to show that writers could come and go in some freedom. Then he realized that the subsequent revolution made nonsense of some kind of Czechoslovakian revenge.

His phone rang. It was Gudgeon in Ottawa, responding to his request to find out about Jaroslav Hasek.

"Staff Inspector," Gudgeon began. "I thought when I left Toronto the last time, you and I had a pretty good understanding."

Salter was baffled. "About what?"

"I thought we were cooperating on this case of yours. I was happy to cover the international scene for you even though it was pretty clearly not our baby."

"What are you talking about?" Salter said. "I mean, what the hell is the matter?"

"Jaroslav Hasek, that's what. You got me to send a signal to our people in Prague."

"Right. So what happened?"

"I think you know that."

"Look, Gudgeon, you're pissed off about something, but I don't know what."

"I think you do."

"Try me. Tell me what I've done."

"All right. Have your fun. I got a call this morning about Hasek. You know who he is, don't you?"

"The guy who mugged Diamond."

"He's been dead for about seventy years."

"Who?"

"You really don't know?" Gudgeon sounded slightly less hostile.

"Listen, I don't know what the hell you're talking about. Now tell me, so I can apologize."

"Okay. Jaroslav Hasek is a very famous Czech writer who wrote a book called *The Good Soldier Schweik*. And if you didn't know that, that makes two of us, but we are the only ones that don't. Right now our organization is looking pretty foolish to the External Affairs crowd. The fucking joke of Ottawa."

"Oh, Christ. What can I say? Blame me. Who would you like me to talk to, to tell them it's me who's stupid, illiterate, whatever?"

"And me."

"I'm sorry, but you can see what happened. That kid gave a false name to the hospital, the first one he could think of. I'll write you a note apologizing for my stupidity, something you can show around. Okay? In the meantime," he continued hurriedly, "if you can trust me, I have another name I'd like you to check. This one I'm certain is real." He waited for a response, but Gudgeon waited, too, so he continued. "Fisher went to Czechoslovakia once, and while he was there, he talked a lot to his interpreter. After he came back, he wrote an article for a Los Angeles paper about it. What I'm wondering is if Fisher was set up in some way. He says this interpreter got drunk and spilled the beans on life under the Communist government. Apparently he was going to be married soon, and he was feeling pretty happy. Could you check it out for me? I don't know what I'm asking, but if a Czech kid mugs Diamond, then gives a false name to the hospital, and then Fisher gets killed, there may be a connection, and the only lead I have is this article. The article was published in a major newspaper. If Fisher had made a fool of himself I would have heard about it when I heard of the article. I'm certain Fisher believed he was writing the inside story.''

"If this backfires, it'll be the last time."

"I told you I was sorry. There's egg on my face, too."

"Yes, but you don't give a shit, do you?"

No, thought Salter. I'm just a dumb Toronto cop. A hick. He now felt some compassion for Gudgeon, deafened by the noise of hee-haws from the culture division of External Affairs. "Not much," Salter confessed.

SIXTEEN

Two DAYS LATER, as Salter was sitting down to breakfast, he got a call from Crabtree asking him to meet him and Josef Hodek at the film-processing lab on Adelaide Street. The lab had just called Crabtree to tell him that the rushes of the previous day's film were not available because one of the cans of film that had been delivered to the lab the night before was blank.

He found Hodek and Crabtree standing on the sidewalk outside the laboratory. Crabtree was unshaven and looked, Salter thought, as though he should be handcuffed to a tree before he killed someone. Hodek looked ten years older, as if he had taken some of Crabtree's pain on himself.

Crabtree said, "The only other people who could be involved are the cameraman and his assistant who brought the film in. I told them to meet us in Oakville. Let's go out in your car. We can talk on the way."

Salter wondered how much control Crabtree had left. Not enough, he judged, if it should become clear who had perpetrated the latest outrage and the culprit was found within reach.

Hodek got in the back, and Crabtree took the passenger seat. As Salter made his way down onto the Gardiner Expressway, Crabtree said, "Tell him the procedure, Josef."

Hodek leaned forward to talk over Salter's shoulder. "Every day we send the cans of film we have shot that day to the processing lab. They make them ready for us to look at the next day. Yesterday, when they opened one can, the film was blank.''

"Exposed?"

"No, unexposed."

"Somebody switched it?"

"That's right," Crabtree said. "Somebody switched it between Oakville and the lab."

"You're sure? It couldn't have got switched in the lab?"

"There's no point in looking for it in the lab. Those guys know their job, and it's the one thing they have to guard against. I won't bother you with the details, and maybe you'll have to do your own check in the end, but their procedures for not making mistakes are watertight. They received it from our guy. It had the proper tape on it marked 'Exposed,' and they opened it right away. It was unexposed. There's three of them involved in the procedure, so there'd have to be a major conspiracy or Houdini trick to switch cans and reidentify them under their noses. The problem is at our end. Tell him about the flat tire, Josef. Christ, I wish I still smoked."

"How reliable is your man, Josef?" Salter interrupted before he could begin. "The one who had to deliver the film."

"Totally, utterly, completely," Josef said. "He has been with me on two films before. We are teaching him, and he is going to be good. He is out of the question."

"Where's he from?"

"Winnipeg, I think. Yes, Winnipeg."

"What's his name?"

"MacDonald. Stuart MacDonald."

"Canadian?"

"His grandfather was in the Mounties."

"What's this all about?" Crabtree wanted to know.

Salter ignored the question. "Do you still have the keys to the house?" he asked. They had dropped down now to Lakeshore Boulevard, driving back along the route of the car chase.

"They're mine until the end of next week. We still have some second-unit stuff to shoot."

Salter pulled into the side street and parked outside Hauser/Vigor's house. There Paul Tessier, Carole Banjani, and Stuart MacDonald, the assistant cameraman, were waiting for them.

"I didn't figure you'd need Diamond or Vigor," Crabtree said. "But we can get them or anyone else you want if we have to."

"I'll start with Josef," Salter said. When nobody moved, he said, "Leave us alone, will you, Jack. Would you come up to the front seat, Josef?"

He could have left Crabtree in the car, but his main point was to impress Crabtree that he was taking the thing as seriously as Crabtree. He was saying, I'm interviewing suspects. It worked. Crabtree looked at Salter in a mild double take, nodded, and got out of the car, then took it upon himself to keep the others back so they couldn't overhear what Salter and Josef were saying.

"Right, Josef. Tell me what happened from the moment you stopped filming."

"Let me explain the procedure first. We used seven cans of film yesterday. Each can is loaded into the camera in a magazine. As we use each reel, we take off the magazine and put on a fresh one. Stuart then takes the magazine into the camera truck, where there's a little darkroom. There he unloads the film, puts it in a can, and labels it 'Exposed.' Now, as soon as we stopped filming, Stuart took away the last magazine, unloaded it, then took all seven reels of exposed film to my car. When he got to the car, he found he had a flat tire. He came back to the set and told us, and Bill gave him his car keys, and Stuart transferred the film to Bill's car and took it to the lab."

"This is standard? I mean, this is the usual routine on any film."

"No, it isn't. I'm working with a skeleton crew be-cause—because Jack doesn't have much money. So not everyone is a union man, and I am personally do-ing things I would never do on a big-budget film. Normally, I would never worry myself about the stock—the film."

"Who has access to the truck where the darkroom is?"

"Stuart has the only key."

"Why does he use your car?"

"He doesn't have a car, so most days he uses mine to take the film to the lab. Then he takes the car to my house, and I get a ride back with someone who lives nearby. Usually, Bill. Yesterday Stuart came back to tell me about the flat tire, to ask me where the spare was. I have a little Renault, and the tire is stored be-side the engine in the front, and Stuart couldn't see it. But I thought it would take too much time, so we used Bill's car. Afterward, Bill and I changed my tire, and I gave him a lift home."

"Why didn't anyone tell me?"

"It was just a flat tire."

"Did you have a look at it? Was it slashed?"

"There was nothing wrong with it that I could see."

"Have you had it fixed?"

"It was last night only. It is still in the trunk."

"I'll have our garage look at it. When MacDonald came back, where was the film?"

"He left it in my trunk and came back to find out how to change my tire."

"How long was he away?"

"About twenty minutes, half an hour, I should think. He tried to drive my car before he heard what was wrong, so that would have taken a few minutes."

"You really sure of MacDonald?"

"Absolutely."

"And you had your eye on the film from the time it left the camera until you gave it to MacDonald."

"Every moment. None of my crew touched it."

"Okay, then what?"

"When Stuart came back, I went down with him. The tire was flat, all right. So we took the film out of the trunk of my car, and Stuart put it in Bill's car and drove off."

"Where were you parked?"

"Both of us on the next street. If you drive around, I will show you."

"I'll go over there with MacDonald. Okay, Josef. Bring Tessier over, will you?"

Tessier had nothing to add. With the help of Josef as translator, he confirmed the other's account, adding that there was no one else around while the film was being transferred to MacDonald. MacDonald was next. Within a few minutes, Salter was as sure of him as Hodek was. The boy was appalled at what had happened, blaming himself for not having locked the trunk of Hodek's car. "But I didn't plan to leave the car until I'd delivered the film," he added. "That's the way it always is. I grab the film, and I just take off."

Salter drove around to the next street and got MacDonald to point out where the car was parked. Then he told MacDonald to walk back to the house, hang around for as long as he thought it had taken him to explain about the flat tire and to collect Connor's keys, and come back to Salter's car. He reappeared in fifteen minutes.

Salter asked all the obvious questions. He drove around the block back to the house and spoke to Crabtree. "There's no point in keeping these people hanging around," he said, indicating Carole Banjani and the cameramen.

There was the possibility that the thief had dumped the film immediately, and Salter radioed for help with a search. While they were waiting, he arranged for Hodek, Tessier, and MacDonald to leave their fingerprints at police headquarters just in case the film was found.

"How much is it going to cost you?" he asked Crabtree.

"Forty thousand dollars."

"Can you make it up?"

"Every time the question is asked, I get closer to saying no. But I'm not finished yet. Believe it or not, the actual shooting is going well. Bill is very economical, and I'm saving a lot of what these bastards are costing me."

"Who else knew the routine for delivering the film to the lab? About MacDonald using Josef's car and all?"

"Just about everybody. It wasn't a secret," Crabtree said. "The only one you can rule out is Fisher. And that girl Helena. I fired her two days ago."

"What for?"

"She was causing trouble." Crabtree made it clear by turning his back that the subject was closed.

FOUR POLICE ARRIVED, and Salter told them what to look for. They divided the area up and began the search. There was nothing else to do, and it was supposed to be everybody's day off, so Salter drove Crabtree and Hodek back to Front Street, where he picked up Hodek's tire and delivered it to the police garage.

LATER IN THE afternoon the searchers reported they had found nothing, and the police garage reported they could find nothing wrong with Hodek's tire, which was now holding air perfectly. The assumption had to be that someone had let the air out.

Now, finally, Ranovic came into his own. He had been useful in a negative way all along because he had totally ingratiated himself with the other drivers and the crew he had come into contact with, but he had heard and seen nothing suspicious. And the gossip he heard was helpful. But now he had been there when it happened.

"I parked at eight o'clock," he said. "And I had a totally boring day. It was hot, remember, and the Winnebago was air conditioned, so I just sat in the cab watching the birds. I saw the whole thing. Hodek's car was half a block down the street—it was already there when I parked—and I would swear that no one went near it all day. You know why I'm sure? Because when that kid MacDonald came along and put the film in the trunk, that was *exciting* after watching pigeons all day. Then I saw him come back and change the film into the other car and take off. I walked down to Hodek's car and saw the problem, but I didn't think about it until you called me. I didn't see anyone around that car all day, certainly not letting the air out of his tires. And I sure as hell didn't see anyone around the car while MacDonald was away."

"Were you watching every minute of the day?"

"I was there. I looked at the sky. I went for a leak. I ate my lunch. But I was there all day."

"You had your eye on Hodek's car all the time while MacDonald was away?"

Ranovic sighed. "I may've talked to Derek and Neville for a minute. Just a minute."

"Then whoever switched the film must have known you were there. Someone knows you're a cop."

"Not by me they don't."

THAT EVENING, Salter told Annie the story of the missing can of film and ended the story by laying out his worries.

"This could be bad," he said. "When I put Vigor and Diamond under protection, I figured that was the real threat taken care of. I forgot this is a film, and if you want to sabotage a film, the most vulnerable part is the film itself. Why didn't I think of that? The fire should have told me."

"Their own standard procedures must have looked good," Annie offered.

"Their procedures are designed to make sure the film doesn't get lost, nothing else. You know, it's like— Ah, shit." Analogies failed him.

"At least you can investigate something now."

"How do you mean?"

"All the other stuff has been kind of vague, hit-and-run kind of thing. Anyone in Toronto might have done them. This time, surely, it can only be one of a few people.''

Salter thought about this. "The trouble is, though, I still don't know enough. Josef explained it all to me, how they handle the film, but I couldn't follow it well enough to ask questions. I need an expert, someone off the set, someone who knows about film.''

Annie said, "What about Dennis Sculler?''

"Who's he?''

"One of Canada's best cameramen.''

"And?''

"He's here. In town. I know him. Maybe he could give you an hour.''

Annie's old job had lapped at the edges of Toronto's artistic community, because almost everyone in her company wanted to write a novel or make a feature film. Occasionally, against the odds, one of them would hoard enough energy to get something done.

"An hour would be enough," Salter said. "I took good notes from Josef. Your guy might just point me in the right direction. How soon?''

Annie went into the kitchen to phone, and Salter got out his notebook and tried to memorize the responses that Hodek and MacDonald had given to his questions. Annie returned in five minutes, looking pleased with herself.

"Mr. Sculler will see you for lunch tomorrow," she said, mimicking a secretary. "Sutton Place at twelve o'clock.''

"Why there?''

"That's where they drink this year.''

"He must be a great admirer of yours.''

"He's bored. He wants to go home, but he has to stay over for a meeting. He did try to date me when he remembered who I was, so when I told him what you wanted, he could hardly say he was busy. He didn't mind. He's intrigued at the idea of helping the cops, too."

"What's he look like?"

Annie considered. "The last time I saw him, he had a leather jacket and jeans, but he's a very gentle guy. Look for a biker priest."

THE NEXT DAY, Salter made his way to the Sutton Place Hotel, where he identified Dennis Sculler waiting for him in the coffee shop. They exchanged civilities, chiefly a gracious acceptance by Salter of Sculler's admiration of Annie's "smarts," as Sculler called them. Then Salter went through his account of the film-switching incident.

Having rehearsed it several times, he was beginning to understand what he was saying, but Sculler made him go through it twice before he accepted that Salter had got it straight. Then he gave the policeman a list of seven or eight questions that Salter hadn't asked. Did MacDonald lock the camera truck every time he used it? Who was responsible for the film stock, with such a tiny crew? Where was the blank stock kept during the day?

But when he had performed this service, he gave it as his opinion that there wasn't much point in avoiding the obvious: Someone had deflated Hodek's tires, then, when MacDonald's back was turned, switched the film in the trunk of the car.

Sculler had a lot more questions to ask about the production; he knew almost everyone involved in it, including his counterpart, Hodek, whom he admired as a professional and liked, as well. But here, too,

Salter could only tell Sculler what he had seen, not what it meant; he felt like a Martian trying to describe the trading floor of the stock exchange to his friends back home, and Sculler soon gave up trying to find out whether Crabtree and Hodek were doing anything interesting or unusual.

As Salter was paying the bill, Sculler said, "Crabtree must be desperately short of money. I've never heard of a director of photography running errands with the film. Doesn't Josef have a focus puller or a clapper/loader? He has to. One thing, though. It makes it easy for you because this film has to have been stolen from the trunk. Whoever did it could not have operated under Josef's eye." He stood up. "Give my love to Annie."

"Thanks," Salter said. "I will." And added, "You, too," because he was thinking so hard he did not know what he was saying.

SEVENTEEN

BACK ON THE SET, Salter had time to corner Ranovic and ask a question that had been on his mind. "Why was Helena fired? What kind of trouble was she causing?"

"Derek says that Carole Banjani made Crabtree get rid of her."

"Why?"

"Banjani thinks that Crabtree was screwing her, and Crabtree had to fire the girl just to prove he wasn't, for a quiet life."

"That's kind of rough on the kid, isn't it? Does Derek think so?"

"No, he doesn't. He thinks someone is tattling in Banjani's ear, trying to stir things up. Crabtree's reaction shows you the pressure he's under. Crabtree's not a bad guy, Derek says, but right now he's not about to worry whether he's being fair or not. He needs a happy Banjani more than he needs a fourth A.D. Now I gotta go."

Later, Salter took the opportunity to let Annie know that her ridiculous worries were over. He used Seth to get the message across. "By the way," he said. "I forgot to tell you. Your girlfriend Helena has been fired."

Seth reared back, blushed, said, "I wondered where she was. What do you mean, 'my girlfriend'?" Then, "What for?"

Salter considered his terms. "Someone thought she was misbehaving."

Annie looked at them both and rose from the table. "One of you make the coffee and bring me some out in the garden." She had seen that Salter and Seth had something to talk about that she could hear about later. As she left, Salter realized it, too. Calling Helena Seth's girlfriend had been a joke, but, to his own discomfort, he had scored a hit.

Again he had to choose his terms carefully. He remembered an old sergeant who worked with him some years before telling him how his father had suddenly decided that his son was of age and began to swear in front of him. At sixteen, the son had been unprepared and slightly shocked. Salter didn't know Seth well enough; he didn't want to do the same thing. "Did *you* think she was easy?" he finished.

"No way." Seth shook his head violently.

"How do you know?"

Seth's blush deepened.

There'll be steam coming off him soon, Salter thought.

"Did you make a move on her?" Was that right? Or was it "put a move"? Or "put a make"? How did they say it now?

Seth gathered his dignity together. "I thought she was terrific, and I thought . . ."

Then Salter realized what the attraction was, and it was not so far from his own. "Her being foreign?"

"I thought . . ."

"Did you know how old she was?"

Seth tumbled off his small dignified perch and turned red again. "When she told me, I thought she was about eighteen or nineteen. She was twenty-five."

"So you gave up."

"Well, sure. Twenty-five! But she wasn't running around. No way. Sherriff thought he had rights, you could tell, but she kept him away."

Salter stood up and started to put the coffee together. "That's too bad, Seth." Then he couldn't resist it. "I mean, it looked perfect. The experienced European woman... What better initiation for a nice Canadian boy."

Seth, in the dusk of the kitchen now reduced to a double row of white teeth in a dark red face, said, "Screw you, Pop."

WHEN SALTER TOLD Annie the substance of their conversation, she said, "Well, well, well. No, I won't say a word. Don't tell me I was wrong. I wasn't. But it doesn't matter now." And then, "You know, at this stage, Seth reminds me of what Hardy said about Tess. Did you ever read it? Something about all the ages coming together in her—the playful child, the mind of a young girl, and the body of a young woman, but all Alec D'Urberville saw was the ripe young woman. What you've got in Seth is a horny young man inside what looks like a schoolboy, and what your Helena saw was the schoolboy. Would that be right? I'm sorry I missed her."

There was still some useful work Salter could be doing on the domestic front for Burnley. Salter put the charge slips into date sequence and made up a tour for himself.

The first was the least hopeful, a Swiss chain restaurant in Yorkville. He knew the restaurant, having acquired a taste for rosti potatoes there, but he was fairly sure that asking them to remember someone two weeks before would be hopeless. He found the waiter who had taken the order, but when he made his request, the waiter simply looked tired at the idea of thinking his way back over three hundred customers. He moved on to a slightly more upscale restaurant on Queen Street with the same result and went on to the next. He noticed that by putting the bills in date order the restaurants were getting more expensive. The third restaurant should have remembered Fisher. It was the kind of establishment that placed a premium on fuss—talking waiters, a pepper mill the size of a human head, and octagonal colored plates that disappeared when the food arrived. But Salter drew a blank here, too.

The fourth one Salter knew. It was a place much favored by politicians, who reserved permanent tables, a restaurant where, if you weren't part of the establishment, even if you had a reservation, they made you wait in a basement room where you listened to four cooks arguing about union problems. This at least had been Salter's single experience of the place when he had been taken there by a nephew of Annie's, a visitor from out of town, who had made the mistake of asking someone in New York to recommend the best restaurant in Toronto. Nevertheless, the place prided itself on knowing who the movers and shakers were, and they might just remember Fisher. He showed the maître d' Fisher's picture, and he remembered him immediately, and his guest: Porter Williams, the guarantor. Salter filed that away carefully and moved on to the last restaurant on his list.

This was a place called Ron and Tony's, where Salter was whisked into the manager's office, apparently because he conflicted with the decor. On his way through the restaurant, he thought he passed both Ron and Tony chatting with the customers; in the back room he waited, and Ron or Tony appeared to deal with him.

"All I can tell you, Officer, is that he was not one of our friends. We know two-thirds of the people we serve. I'm surprised he got in; we only take reservations from people who are recommended by friends."

"I imagine he was well connected. He was a scriptwriter from Hollywood."

"Ah, then. He probably dropped a name. We can't check up on everybody. But I try to meet all our guests, and I can't remember him."

"Maybe Tony met him."

"There is no Tony. Or Ron, either, for that matter. That's just a name. I own the restaurant. My name is Harold."

On his way out, Salter wondered what the basic food was in a place like this. It wasn't French or Italian. Nor was it upper-class Canadian, like the previous place. Ron and Tony's was decorated in patio colors, light green and lavender and pink, a color scheme that continued into the plates, which were edged in black. He imagined that the washroom in the basement would be equally tastefully decorated.

Salter reported back to Burnley—he was beginning to want to be scrupulous about touching base with Homicide on every detail—and suggested that he take the specific problem of Fisher's dinner companions back to the set and also check up on Williams. Burnley agreed, and Salter drove out to Oakville and went the rounds of the obvious people who might have known where and with whom Fisher had eaten dinner while he was there. The best he could come up with was that Fisher claimed to have a lot of contacts in town and was probably hustling another movie idea that he wasn't sharing with anyone on the set. He had asked Crabtree to recommend some good, quiet restaurants, and Crabtree responded with the last one on Salter's list. Fisher had reported back that he thought it was overpriced but hadn't said who he had been dining with.

Now Salter found Porter Williams's card and put in the call. Williams agreed that he had dined once with Fisher.

"Why?"

"I think you know that, Staff Inspector."

"He invited you, though. He paid."

"That's right. The restaurant was my suggestion. I keep a table there. But you're right. He invited me."

"Why?"

"We had made some contact earlier. He knew who I was."

"So what did you talk about?"

"Let's not be childish. I have only one interest in that movie."

Salter waited.

Sighing, Williams continued. "He wanted to let me know that if I had to take over the film, he was available for any work that needed to be done. You are aware of his special interest in the project?"

"He saw it as his baby."

"Apparently."

"Did he tell you he didn't think Crabtree could complete the film on time?"

"That was his opinion."

"Did he tell you about the troubles?"

"He brought me up-to-date."

"Did he have any idea who was causing them?"

"He seemed to think that Crabtree had enemies. He did. Fisher."

"And what was your reaction?"

"I made a note of it."

"That all? We're conducting a murder investigation, Mr. Williams. We could meet in my office."

"Are you pushing me? This call is being recorded. All my calls are."

"Great. You won't have to write this down, then. I want a meeting with you, in your office or mine. Today."

"What, exactly, do you want to know?"

"I want to know what you did about Fisher's information. Did you pass it on?"

"I spoke to Jack Crabtree. That was when he suggested I see you."

"You told him that it was Fisher you had been talking to?"

"Yes."

"You realize what this means? This is important information."

"Which I'm now giving you, at your request. This is your inquiry, Staff Inspector, but I can imagine the implications."

"Can you?"

"Of course. Jack Crabtree would be very angry."

"Did Fisher ask to speak to you confidentially?"

"Of course."

"But you didn't keep the confidence."

"You know why I didn't."

"Tell me."

"It was obvious from the start that Mr. Fisher regarded himself as a very clever man. That being the case, he might have thought he was fooling me, but I had to consider the possibility that it was Fisher himself who was Crabtree's enemy.''

"And you told Crabtree this?"

"No, I didn't. That might get me into trouble. I told Crabtree the facts. He's not a fool. I knew he would protect himself. I understand Fisher didn't have access to the set after that."

"All right, Mr. Williams. I'll get back to you."

"You still want that interview?"

"I'll be in touch."

"Right you are."

IT WAS TIME to go back to Crabtree and Banjani.

The two policemen talked to them one at a time.

Carole Banjani was defiant—and afraid. They took her first over the time she had spent with Crabtree when Fisher was killed. Step by step they made her spell out what she and Crabtree had eaten, where they sat in the restaurant, what they had talked about, and the route home. She hesitated occasionally, but only in the natural way of remembering. Then he came to Helena Sukos.

"To the best of my knowledge that girl was sleeping with everybody on the set," Banjani said.

"What was your knowledge?"

"I knew that she was after Jack."

"And Sherriff, too? And Fisher?"

Banjani blushed and spat out, "Probably."

"You didn't know?"

"I was pretty sure."

"I don't think you were sure at all. I think you told Sherriff that so he wouldn't be too upset when Crabtree fired Helena."

"Helena, is it? You soft on her, too?"

"Was that it?"

"The sooner Miss Sukos was gone, the better."

"And who cares who gets hurt in the process? Including Miss Sukos. And maybe Fisher, too. All this poisonous shit you've been spilling could lead us back to Fisher's killer and the reason he was killed. You know that?"

It was risky stuff, but only Burnley was listening.

"I didn't make it up about her and Jack," she cried. "Of course Jack denies it, but I got it from a good source."

"Who? Justify yourself, Miss Banjani."

"Josef Hodek, that's who."

The breath went out of Salter. "Josef?" he said quietly. "Josef?"

Banjani grabbed her advantage. "That's right. Josef. Everybody trusts him, don't they? I did. He told me that girl was a real trouble maker and that if I wanted to hang on to Jack, I should make him get rid of her."

"Josef?"

"That's right." It was said now; she had breached a major confidence, and it freed her to use the information for its full effect. "Josef asked me to please not say he had told me because he felt a little responsible for her. Apparently he had put in a good word for her with Sherriff, so he wanted her to go away, but he didn't want her to know it was anything to do with him. But I don't think I should be kept to that if you're looking for a murderer," she ended piously.

With a feeling in his gut as if he had swallowed a stone, Salter began thinking about Josef Hodek.

"A bit rough on Helena if she wasn't involved with Jack, isn't it?"

"Oh, the hell with Helena. If she wasn't screwing Jack, she soon would have been. I know him."

"I guess you do, Miss Banjani. All right. Thanks."

With Crabtree, they went once more over his dinner with Banjani on Sunday night. It corresponded in all the important details with Banjani's version, and Crabtree only needed time to remember in order to corroborate the whole story. Salter came to the guarantor.

"You had good reason to squash Fisher, didn't you, Jack?"

Crabtree said promptly, "Williams called me. I know what you're after. Sure, I'd've killed Fisher, in a manner of speaking, but I wouldn't have *killed* him, and I didn't, did I? Apart from plotting behind my back, or so he thought, he didn't do me any harm. He didn't beat up Diamond, and I don't think he was involved in any of the other stuff."

"Why didn't you tell me about Fisher's involvement with Williams?"

"Because he was wasting his time, and I had enough on my plate. I didn't want to confuse you. I could handle Fisher, and I was planning to."

"How?"

"By making sure he never worked on a film in this country again. And maybe in the States."

Salter let him go. By now he was avoiding his real concern.

"Now," Burnley said, "we have to talk to"—he looked at his notes—"Josef Hodek."

"Yeah, I guess we do."

Burnley held up a cigarette, silently asking Salter's permission. He lit up, carefully blowing the smoke up and away from Salter, placed the cigarette on the edge of the table farthest away from the staff inspector, and pulled his chair an inch closer to the table. "This movie of yours is like a giant rock, you know that? Every time you lift it, somebody else crawls out. Let's talk to Hodek. I don't think I remember him from the first time around."

"We interviewed him. He didn't want any trouble. Sees no evil, hears no evil."

"This kid, Helena Sukos, wouldn't agree about speaking no evil, though."

Salter had had time now to get over his alarm, time to realize they had to know why Hodek had gotten rid of Helena. "Okay, let's bring him in."

Burnley asked the questions. Hodek was wary, polite, and formal with both of them, and Salter saw immediately that the photographer no longer trusted him. Hodek was once more being interrogated by the police. For a man with his background, that was enough.

Burnley took him over the same ground he had covered before, getting Hodek to say again that he was not aware of any enmities on the set beyond those obvious to everybody. Then he came to Helena Sukos. Why did Hodek advise Banjani to get rid of her?

"I thought it would be better if she was sent away. There were too many personal problems with the film, and Helena would cause more, I thought. She is a nice girl, but not someone to be near Mr. Crabtree with Carole watching."

"Did you know this kid was sleeping around?"

"I knew she was too available."

"How?"

"By the best way I could know. Myself. She was very ambitious, and she might think it was a way to advance."

"Anybody else?"

"You would have to ask them. I am afraid so."

"Where is she now?"

Hodek shook his head. "She has probably left Toronto."

"She left when Crabtree fired her?"

"No. She was here at least until yesterday, because she was with us, me and my wife, the night before."

"Socializing? With you? After you got her fired?"

"She didn't know I was responsible. I was sorry for her. She was someone to be sorry for, because—what's the phrase?—she was her own worst enemy. I thought she should be sent away, but apart from that, I was sorry for her."

Burnley looked at Salter, who shook his head, and the sergeant thanked Hodek. Salter looked out the window to avoid Hodek's eyes as he left.

Burnley said, "Was she peddling her ass all over the lot? How old is that guy? Sixty?"

"Mid-fifties."

"So he figures if she's offering it to a guy his age, she must be doing the same to Crabtree. That figures?"

"He doesn't want trouble. Maybe he felt she was letting the side down. You know, both being central Europeans. I don't know. You got your answer, anyway."

"I guess so." Burnley took out his cigarettes, then changed his mind and put them back in another pocket. "I think he was lying, you know that?"

"Why?" Now it comes, Salter thought.

"I don't think she went after him at all. I mean, Christ, sixty." Burnley ran a hand over his forty-year-old chin. "I think he was just stamping out a little hanky-panky before it caused trouble around the camera."

Salter said nothing. Burnley sighed. "Another dead end. It looks to me like we go our separate ways now. We haven't made a single connection with the movie crowd, and I'm going to go back to square one. I've got a visiting fireman stabbed in his room for sex or money. This could put a hole in my track record. Was Fisher tight about money?"

"Very, according to his pal from Hollywood."

"Maybe that's it. That's why whores get their money first. The john's not so inclined to haggle before he gets laid as he is after. Maybe Fisher's the exception. There hadn't been any sex, but we don't know what he might have had in his wallet. She could've seen a lot of cash while he was bargaining with her."

"What next?"

"I don't know. We have to wait. We'll get a tip. So"—he stood up abruptly—"let me take you back to town."

On the way back Burnley said, "You don't think there's anything in this Nazi thing?"

"I don't think so, but that's another world. I told you what I've found. I can't connect them up with anyone on the set."

Burnley nodded, irritated, apparently, that the case wasn't simple. "Stay in touch. If there's no more damage to the movie, I guess you're up the creek, too."

"If there's no more damage, then I have to wonder if Fisher was the one, like you said. But who switched the film?"

"Here we go again. I'll let you chase that one around. As I say, keep in touch."

EIGHTEEN

WHEN GUDGEON CALLED BACK, his voice was full of news. "I think I have what you want, Charlie," he began. "It needs a context. You got a few minutes? I'll tell you a little story to try to give you a handle on this."

Salter recognized the signs. Gudgeon was pleased with himself, and the simple delivery of his information was not enough. He was going to dramatize it. That was all right with Salter. He'd get what he wanted, and Gudgeon deserved an admiring audience after his humiliation. "Let me close the door, Hal," he said. Then, "Okay. Go ahead."

"You ready for this? A while ago we sent a university professor to one of the Eastern bloc countries. When he came back, he wrote a piece for one of the Toronto papers, like Fisher's. He attacked what he saw and what he'd heard about, and somehow it got reprinted in the underground press over there, and the government decided to react. So they published an article about him, not referring to the article he wrote, just what a creep they had found him, Fascist, pervert, that kind of stuff. Now, no one who read the piece would understand why they were doing this to him except people who'd read the professor's article. You follow? They didn't want to draw new readers to his article, just discredit him in the eyes of the ones who'd already seen it. What was interesting is that they had all kinds of stuff about his private life, lots of true details that added up to a character assassination. They made him into a real deviate. The piece was full of stuff about how he had recommended killing off the Indians by feeding them cheap liquor, that he didn't speak out about the mistreatment of the Japanese during the war, and how he used to belong to a sailing club that didn't have any Jews in its membership.

"Now, Professor Livingstone analyzed the article, and he told us there was no way they could have written it without interrogating all the people he'd met, a detail he'd told to this person, another to that. We'd talked to Livingstone before he left: He wasn't naive, and he knew all the tricks to avoid, like dealing with fake black-market money changers and so on, but still, after four vodkas he was bound to compare Canada and their country a little bit. It was only polite to admit we had our problems, too. The point is they got stuff from the bus drivers, the guides, the barmen, as well as the local professors he met, so we know they routinely debriefed anyone they saw foreign visitors talking to. Livingstone only wrote what he saw and what he heard. Now, Fisher was in Prague, where half the population was informing on the other half, and obviously someone told him a lot. They would naturally analyze Fisher's article and find out who he might have been talking to. Officially, they ignored the article, but we have reason to believe that they didn't ignore Fisher's sources, one of whom was his interpreter." Gudgeon paused. A revelation, a climax, was coming. "We find it highly circumstantial that the guy who acted as Fisher's interpreter went to jail for eight months just after the article appeared."

"What was he charged with?"

"Offenses against the state. It was a secret trial."

"What was his name."

"Jiri Hof."

"Thanks." Salter looked at the name for a few moments. Then he remembered Fisher mentioning it on the set at St. Lawrence Market. "Okay. Now I've got another request. Can you find out who Jiri Hof's friends were, his relatives?"

"I'll ask our sources in West Germany. They keep tabs on everything that goes on."

"Thanks. I'm very grateful. It's very unlikely that this will lead to anything, but I need to cover every base."

"Sure you do. I understand. A lot of our work's like that. You build it up a brick at a time, then, bingo, you can see the whole picture. I'll get on to it right away."

Gudgeon reported back with a list of names of Jiri Hof's relatives and associates, those that were known to his Czech sources. "Any of those mean anything?" he asked.

"None at all," Salter said.

"Sorry."

"No, no, Hal. That's good," Salter said. And meant it.

AT FOUR O'CLOCK the next morning, Salter heard the *Globe and Mail* land on his porch, and he remembered that he had never found the car that was involved in the swastika incident. An image of a car cruising the silent streets of Oakville formed in his mind and stayed there.

He had been awake all night looking for an alternative solution or a doubt that he could build into one. Gudgeon's last call had given him some hope, but only enough to allow him not to come to the conclusion that was forcing itself on him until he had investigated all the alternatives. He had no doubt now that Fisher's death and the sabotage were parts of the same problem, but so far he had no proof, either. He went through the problem again and again, looking always for the details that would make such proof impossible, that would seem to prove the opposite.

He came again to the switched reel of film. He tried to imagine himself as the culprit waiting on the street late that afternoon for MacDonald to appear with the seven cans of film, put them in the trunk of Hodek's car, discover the flat tire, and return to the set; then, moving to the car, opening the trunk, exchanging one of the reels, and returning with the reel of film to—where?—to his own car, to stash the film until he could dispose of it. For about five minutes, at least, he would be in full daylight with a can of film under his arm. The risk would have been enormous. And Ranovic had seen no one like that. The only possible answer in the end was MacDonald himself, but then why all the foofaraw with flat tires? All MacDonald had to do was drive off somewhere, switch the reels, and the job was done. Ponderously, the answer came to this: MacDonald had constructed a clever smokescreen. In seeming to look at Hodek's flat tire, he could have let the air out and then returned to the set, thus creating the scenario they had all swallowed.

Now Salter began again, with MacDonald in mind, tried to see him arriving at the car, putting the film in the trunk, then going through the motions of emptying the tire of air, and Salter saw Ranovic move in to offer to help. Salter worked at imagining someone else letting the air out of the tire, saw that Ranovic was not there because it was early morning, and realized that the tire had been flat all day. He came once more to the image he had awakened with and the knowledge he had been trying to avoid. Now he knew who had let the air out of the tire. Now he thought he knew where to look for the film.

THE FILM LABORATORY did not open until nine. At eight-thirty, Salter called in to the offices of Balmuto Productions and got the keys of the Oakville house from Fay, Crabtree's secretary, then drove down to Adelaide Street hoping, still, for a hole in his new understanding.

"WHEN THE FILM ARRIVES," the technician at the lab said, "the front window issues a receipt and takes it back to the developing room right away, where he gets a lab guy to sign for it. That day it was me. See?" He pointed to his signature, one of a line of names. "Then I began developing it."

"Wouldn't you know the film was blank?"

"Don't say blank. Say 'unexposed' or 'exposed.' It could be exposed and blank. Look, I'll show you." He took Salter into a storage area and showed him a can of film. Around the edge of the can was a strip of white tape with the words UNEXPOSED FILM repeated continuously. "Now, if the film is exposed, it would have this on it." He held up a reel of tape printed with the word EXPOSED.

"Can anyone get hold of this tape?"

"Sure. You can buy it in any film supply house."

"So this can came in with the EXPOSED tape on it."

"That's right, but it wasn't exposed."

Salter left the laboratory and drove along the lake to Oakville. He was still pretending to himself that it was possible that Fisher's death had nothing to do with the sabotage, because the only connection was something he didn't want to think about until it was the last one. He would untangle the threads one at a time, this one first. Never mind where it took him.

HE STARTED ON the street where Hodek had parked his car on the morning the film was switched. First he walked to each end of the block looking, not very hopefully, for something the searchers might have missed, some place a can of film might be stashed, a house for sale, a telephone booth, that would make it impossible to say who had put it there, but there was nothing. The police searchers had been frustrated not because they hadn't found the film but because there was nowhere to look: There are no crannies on an Oakville side street. Thus, if it had been taken from Hodek's car while MacDonald was returning to the house, it had probably been transferred to another car.

Salter let himself into the house and went upstairs to the master bedroom, the location in the film of the Iron Cross. The room had been left intact by the set dressers, and Salter glanced around briefly before beginning his search. He pretended to be Hodek taking the magazine from Tessier and giving it to Mac-Donald. He left the room with the imaginary film under his arm, walked to the head of the stairs, then down to where MacDonald was waiting by the front door. It was ridiculously easy. As he walked along the hall at the head of the stairs, he passed a cupboard, a linen closet in the hall. The door was in two halves, like a stable door, and he opened the top and felt among the slightly disordered towels. The magazine was pushed to the back of the cupboard, but it was easy to reach.

Salter left the house, locked the film in the trunk of his own car, and went back to town.

HE HAD TO MAKE a call to Gudgeon. The previous call had been inadequate, now that he had the name.

Gudgeon, reassured against Salter's perfidy, was once more on his side. "Josef Hodek. I'll go back to our people in West Germany. You'll have to wait until tomorrow again because of the time zones."

Then, "Negative," Gudgeon reported the next day. "Hof was two years old when Hodek left Czechoslovakia. Hof is from Bratislava. No connection at all."

"Good," said Salter. "Thanks."

So perhaps there was some other explanation, or perhaps it wasn't just personal. Josef would tell him, no doubt.

SALTER HAD TWO MORE questions, and he waited on the set until he could get MacDonald on his own and ask him.

"I was," MacDonald said immediately. "I'm always the first on the set. Of the camera crew, that is."

"You're sure of it? Think about it: When you walked into the room where you were going to set up, there was no one there?"

"No, I'm sure."

"But you weren't the first of the crew to arrive, were you?"

"Oh, no, some of the trucks were there."

"Was Mr. Crabtree there? Carole Banjani? Sherriff?"

"Not Sherriff, that's for sure. No, none of them. Just some technicians I couldn't put a name to. I remember that new kid, the one who replaced the girl who was fired. I think she'd been there for about two hours in case she was late. Oh, and Josef. He'd got there early, too, and he was talking to the new kid, helping her over her nervousness, the way he does."

"No one else? Who came in after you?"

"Paul, the camera operator, and then they all appeared."

Now Salter decided to lay down some smoke. "The new kid? Where did she come from?"

"Sherriff found her somewhere."

"Was she around when they were unloading the camera?"

"Not that I remember. She might have been."

"And each of those seven magazines you took straight from the camera to the darkroom and locked yourself in, and you're sure you left it locked afterward."

"Certain. That door won't close unless you lock it. And yes, I took each of the magazines from either Paul or Josef."

"As they took them off the camera?"

"Once I'd got sent off on an errand, and I missed the changeover, so Josef was waiting for me with the magazine when I came back."

"Waiting for you? Where?"

"By the front door of the house, I think. Why?"

"Don't get offended, son; I just have to make sure that no one made a silly mistake. But from what you tell me, I can be sure that the film went missing from the trunk of Josef's car while you were off getting Bill Connor's car keys, can't I?"

Hodek was approaching, and Salter broke off, but from a few yards away he saw MacDonald evidently telling Hodek what had transpired between him and Salter, complete with gestures of mild disbelief and head-shaking ridicule. He hoped that the subject was the dumbness of Toronto's cops.

HE HAD ENOUGH evidence to proceed to formal questioning, and the rest would come. Trundling some pictures around the restaurants would do it. It would not be hard to turn suspicion into certainty. When you have a suspect, it's easy; easier, anyway, than when you don't. Then what? He considered again the path he would have to travel to confirm his suspicions, the doors he would have to open. Now he knew, but he did not yet know what he was going to do about it.

Twice before, Salter had been on cases where he had felt some sympathy for the convicted man. Neither crime had been premeditated, and in each case Salter had been glad that the result had been a minimum sentence for manslaughter. This was the first time he had met and known and liked the killer before the crime had been committed. He thought he understood how events had led to this end. He had no proof, of course. Certainty, but no proof. He could gather that at leisure.

And yet if he should step back from it, who else would be able to pick up the thread? And he started down the most dangerous path of all, the "what if?" road. It wasn't a matter of doing anything that could rebound against him. It was a matter of doing nothing, of failing, of appearing stupid. Could he stand that? And if there was something he had overlooked so that others could succeed where he had failed, what then? Could he stand that, too? All this was just crazy fantasy, of course, the thinking of a poor man's Sydney Carton. He wasn't serious about it. Still, he could continue fantasizing for a while. He didn't have to make up his mind yet. Let the proof come and he would have no alternative. But not yet. First he would talk to the expert—not the expert criminologist, but the expert at seeing immediately the dangers for Salter in even thinking about this last possibility. He would talk to Orliff. This time he took his rod. He was glad now he hadn't succeeded in putting too much distance between them.

NINETEEN

SALTER SAID, "Do you sleep up here yet?"

They were sitting on the porch Orliff had just finished building. The plywood shell of the cottage was in place and most of the cedar siding. The porch screening was complete, so the two men could sit relatively safe from insects on the lawn chairs that constituted the only furniture so far. Outside, the mosquitoes swarmed, searching for gaps in the screen, but the occasional successful intruder could be killed as soon as it landed. Salter watched one alight on his hand, waited a second for it to get comfortable, then splatted it.

Orliff shook his head. "Too many holes for those little buggers to get through until I get the siding on. I tried sleeping here last week, but I had to get up every half hour to smoke 'em out. I stay at that motel you passed just before the grocery store. Another week, then I can sleep here."

"Your wife come up?"

"She took a look last weekend. She says to let her know when it's fit for humans." Orliff laughed. "By her standards, that'll be sometime next year. But that's all right. How's your drink?"

"I'm fine." Salter shook the can of Fresca to show how full it was. I worked with this guy for eight years, he thought, and I never knew he was a teetotaler. For all I know, he's a born-again Christian. "How's the fishing?"

"Good, they tell me. I haven't had a chance to test it yet. Been waiting for someone like you."

All around the site there were piles of lumber and construction materials. To Salter's eye they represented a lot of work yet to be done, too much, but he had to believe that Orliff was doing what he wanted at last. He seemed happy enough, except that he hadn't gone fishing, which Salter understood was one of the main reasons he was building the cottage. Orliff's whole project bothered him; his instinct was to look for the flaws in this retirement heaven, and he had trouble maintaining an admiring posture. The fact was, as Annie later pointed out to him when he relaxed at home and began to nitpick at Orliff's world, it was Orliff's having yearned and planned for retirement and the further fact that the reality did not seem to be a letdown that bothered Salter. He had no plans for his own retirement, the idea made him nervous, and he tried not to think about it. If pressed, he would have discovered in himself a desire to end his days tottering off to work, toothless and drooling. At some point in the last few years the future had turned into the present, but he wasn't yet ready for it to turn into the past.

Salter shifted his chair back out of the sun and looked out over the lake. It was a beautiful, warm June day; the sun was hot enough to burn, and the lake was calm and inviting, though Salter knew that this early in the year the water would still be too cold for him.

Orliff stood up and swallowed the last of his drink. "Let's go fishing."

THE SPAWNING SEASON was just ending, and Orliff took Salter down to the lake to where a stretch of shoreline looked as if it had been landscaped to create a nesting ground for smallmouth bass, a hundred yards of shallow rocky water overhung by a lip of matted vegetation only a foot above the surface of the lake and sticking out to provide some shade for the edge of the lake underneath.

"This is a bass nursery," Orliff said. "That's what the guy at the marina called it. Let's see." He flicked a tiny red-feathered plug into the water two inches from the shore and reeled in rapidly. The fish struck two feet from shore, jumped clear of the lake, and danced on its tail, flicking its head from side to side, ridding itself of the bait before Orliff could get his hook set properly.

"This is the place," Orliff said happily, adjusting the motor so that the boat was barely moving. He set the course parallel to the shore, about twenty feet away. Salter cast and hooked one right away, a fish big enough to cause Orliff to reel in and concentrate on keeping the boat straight while Salter fought to bring the fish in. Fifteen minutes later, he had a three pound bass gasping in the net.

Orliff said, "That's the biggest smallmouth I've seen in years."

Salter slipped his thumb in the fish's mouth, gripping the thick, rubbery lip, and lifted it clear of the net, unhooking his bait. He held the still-pulsing fish up high.

"It's a keeper," Orliff said.

"I guess."

Just then the fish managed one last fierce convulsion and tore itself out of Salter's grip. It hit the water, lay on its side for a moment, gasping, then turned and dived to the bottom like a flash of black light.

"I guess not," Salter said.

"Son of a bitch," Orliff said, smiling. "You like to eat 'em?"

"Not much."

"Nor do I. Nine times out of ten I take it back to the cottage, leave it around for three days until it starts to stink, then I have to bury it. Fish like that, a real beauty, it's a shame to let it rot." He started up the motor, and they resumed casting. Almost immediately, both men got strikes. They threw the fish back, agreed now, and puttered on. They fished the stretch twice, getting a dozen strikes each, never finding anything as big as Salter's first but hooking several two-pounders. Then it stopped. They tried four more passes but could raise nothing.

"That was what you came for, eh, Charlie?" Orliff said. "Can't promise you action like that every time."

"Why did they stop hitting?"

"I think they realize what's going on. They aren't feeding. They're protecting their spawn, and they'll hit anything that comes near, but I think they learn fast that we aren't something to worry about. Let's fish our way home."

The cottage was about a mile away, a good hour's trolling. When their lines were set, Orliff said, "You making any headway?"

It was the purpose of the afternoon, but when Orliff had seen Salter's rod, he had insisted they fish first.

Now Salter said, "None at all," and knew he had taken the first step.

"Can't you find a connection between Fisher and the other stuff?"

"I've been over it a dozen times. The only way I can see it could be connected is if Fisher had done the damage and Crabtree caught him at it. But Crabtree was with his girlfriend that night. The continuity girl, Carole Banjani. I've tried to get behind their story, but it's watertight."

"I wondered about her. I wondered if she had it in her to avenge Crabtree, something like that."

"So did I. I wouldn't put it past her, but she was with Crabtree, all right."

"Sherriff?"

"He had a reason. But he isn't a killer. And he's got a timed and dated receipt from a bar on Bloor Street for ten minutes after he drove away. And we know when that was from the Gospel-reading cabbie."

"Who else did Fisher cross? Diamond?"

"Diamond was in his room all night. We had a guy sitting in the lobby protecting him."

"Right. That's all Fisher's enemies, I guess."

"There's one other thing that sounds kind of nutty, but I checked it, anyway. Fisher had been to Czechoslovakia, and when he came back, he wrote an article in a Los Angeles paper knocking the system over there. Our CSIS guy figured it might have upset the Czechs, though I don't think he was serious that they were involved. If any major organization had wanted to wreck the film, they could have done it; and if anyone had targeted Fisher from the beginning, they wouldn't have played around so long with fire alarms and swastikas. I figured the only connection with Czechoslovakia was through Hodek."

He had cast the bait; now he had to hope that Orliff would take it.

"Josef?" Orliff asked.

"That's right. He's from Prague. So I asked Ottawa to run a security check on him, and they came up empty. Josef left his home country twenty years ago; he's never tried to go back, and he has very few acquaintances left there now."

"Oh, Christ, no, forget about Josef. He's harmless. So what are you going to do? Keep chewing away at it?"

"Trying to find the troublemaker now is a waste of time. Crabtree is going to be able to complete, and unless someone tries to blow up the set on the last day, that's it. After that, the people working on the movie will be scattered all over the continent."

"And Fisher?"

"Homicide is at a dead end. It wasn't anybody we know on the set. It might have been someone we don't know, a junior technician, say, or a complete outsider."

"A girl?"

"Possible. A whore. Or someone he was meeting secretly—they're pretty sure whoever it was came in the back door. Someone came to get paid."

"The usual, then. If you knew who it was, you'd know why, and if you knew why, you'd know who it was. It sounds to me like an open file."

"How do you mean?" Spell it out, Salter urged, so that you'll remember in two years' time.

"You need a break, but you might not get one for months, if ever, so it stays open. Put it with the open files in Homicide."

"I should forget it?"

"I think so. I know, they're going to tell the world it was your case in the beginning and you fucked up. They'll look good if they solve it, and they won't look bad if they don't. Either way, you aren't going to look good. But look at it this way: It's time you fell on your ass; people will like you better for it, even Homicide. You gave it your best shot. Now it's time to quit. You have to know when you're licked."

"That wasn't what you were saying before."

"I know. But now I think you're stuck."

They reached Orliff's dock and tied the boat up.

"I'll make some coffee, Charlie?"

Salter declined. He wanted a beer, badly. "I've wasted enough time."

They walked up the path to Salter's car. Orliff leaned in the window as Salter started the engine. "Got what you came for, Charlie?"

"Yeah, I guess I did."

Orliff nodded. "Come back when this is over. We'll go after some pickerel."

On the drive home, he went through the whole thing once more. He had satisfied himself about Orliff; the superintendent now believed that he had advised Salter as to the best approach to the case at this point. Now Salter could act, or not. He decided to wait until the end of filming, knowing that simply by postponing his final decision, he was making it. A lot was riding on it, but he could see no more danger. Just one more talk with Burnley.

THE HOMICIDE SERGEANT listened carefully while Salter went through the possibility of a Czech connection: the phone calls to Gudgeon in Ottawa, the article by Fisher, the check on Hodek, the only possible link. At the end he added on his conversation with Orliff.

Burnley sat back looking irritated. "Are we talking about some kind of revenge plot managed from someplace in Bohemia?"

"It's a possibility, but only because the guy who assaulted Paul Diamond gave this name of a dead Czech writer, a joke, like calling yourself Charlie Chaplin, and because Fisher wrote an article once."

"Those are the only reasons?"

Salter heard the emphasis and increased the pressure. "The only ones."

"That sounds to me like a hell of a coincidence."

Salter said nothing.

"I think it's bullshit," Burnley said decisively. "But if it isn't, you know what it's like trying to get those countries behind the curtain to cooperate? We don't have any extradition treaties, and before they had their revolutions, they wouldn't even answer our questions. Once a case went behind the curtain, it was good-bye, baby."

"And now?"

"It should be better." Burnley looked around the room, searching for an exit. "No, it'll be the same. I mean, the people in charge now aren't going to want to help us find one of their heroes, are they?"

Salter said nothing.

"I don't think it's worth bothering with, do you?"

Salter understood that Burnley was looking for support. "If that's your experience, then you're probably right."

"The hell with it. Write me a report, will you, Staff, saying you couldn't find any connection?"

"Sure."

"What about this guy Hodek? He's the only possible connection on the set, isn't he?"

"Like I told you, he hasn't been home for twenty years. The CSIS couldn't find any connection. You met the guy."

"Right. And Orliff thinks we can forget about him?"

"Orliff just laughed at the idea."

Burnley looked relieved. "I'd be chasing geese, then, wouldn't I?"

"Something like that."

"Then let's forget it. I'll keep looking around town. I think I could've been right in the first place. Doig still thinks so."

"A prostitute of some kind?"

Salter could imagine from the awkward silence what kind of conversations had taken place between Burnley and Doig.

Burnley looked at the file. "Yeah, write me that report, though." Then he had a thought. "Hold on. We've ruled out Hodek, but don't pitch the idea of there being *no* connection with Czechoslovakia. See, if I can't find anyone around here, then that may be the reason, and because we can't get any help from the other end, in Czechoslovakia, I mean, I could leave it as the only possibility, couldn't I? We'll drop it, we always do, but it'll be no skin off my nose, will it? So write me that report explaining all that stuff about Fisher's article and leave it as a possibility. How's your investigation going?"

"I think I'm stuck."

Burnley smiled. "I gotta go. Guy just threw his wife off a roof, and we're waiting to see if she dies before we know what to charge him with." He put the Fisher file in a tray and shook hands with Salter. "Nice working with you."

TWENTY

THERE WAS A gloom lying over the set because of the body offstage, and tempers showed even more than usual. It was no surprise, therefore, that there should be an explosion between Crabtree and Sherriff, because once more Sherriff had delivered Vigor late for his scene.

They were there to reshoot the scene of Vigor steering his boat out of the mooring, after "killing" Ranovic, and Diamond scrambling aboard. Connor was unsatisfied with the rushes, and in spite of all the troubles, they had found enough time to do it again.

The call was for 11:00 P.M., in the expectation of getting the camera rolling at midnight. At 1:00 A.M., when everyone else had been waiting for almost two hours, Sherriff arrived with Henry Vigor and his detective, jumped out of the car, and ran toward Crabtree, shouting, "It's okay, they've changed the forecast. We can go ahead."

Crabtree watched Sherriff approach. To those who could read the signals, he had the air of a man who was trying to decide which part of Sherriff to break first. "They changed the forecast?" he repeated, his voice courteous.

"Yeah, there was a small-craft warning, Jack. Didn't you hear? There was no way we could have gone ahead."

The lake had been coated with scum all day. Occasionally, something rippled the surface, but otherwise it was a sheet of dirty-looking mercury.

Sherriff approached within range, mistaking the quietness of Crabtree's voice. When he got close enough, Crabtree jumped. Before anyone could move, he had fallen on Sherriff like a tree and had his hands around the assistant director's throat. By the time he was hauled off, Sherriff was actually choking. "Jesus, Jack," he gasped. "Couldn't you just fire me?"

"Get off this set. If you come close enough to me ever again, I'll throw you under a train. Get out. Now."

It was the first time Salter had seen Sherriff looking abashed. He stroked his neck, smoothed his hair, shrugged, and walked away.

Crabtree put himself together and looked around at the crew. "Where's Diamond?" he asked.

"He's in the Winnebago," Connor said.

The fair-haired boy who had been identified as second assistant director came forward. "I'll look after getting Mr. Diamond, sir."

Crabtree looked at him, trying to remember, then nodded. "You are now the first A.D. Can we manage?"

"I think so. We've still got Gerda."

"Then let's go. Call Diamond. Bill. Let's go."

THE WHOLE SEQUENCE took them to the edge of dawn, and when Bill Connor pronounced himself satisfied for the last time, half the crew simply sat down where they were and waited for some energy to return. Crabtree walked to the sea wall and vomited into the lake.

Salter had stayed close to the action all night, and now, as the camera crew dismantled their gear and the security guard waited to collect the film, he walked over to Josef Hodek, slipped his hand under the photographer's arm, and led him to his car. He wanted to move quietly. Josef offered no resistance and showed no surprise at Salter's gesture, and the two men got into the car. After a minute, Salter said, "Jiri Hof."

Hodek said nothing. He sat still, waiting to be sentenced.

"Jiri Hof," Salter repeated. "A man from Prague who told Fisher what he really thought of the system and as a result Fisher wrote an article and Hof went to jail. Fisher was a prick—you have a Czech word for it?—but killing him was a bit rough, Josef."

Hodek said nothing.

"You knew that Fisher wrote the article."

"I heard about it," Hodek said eventually, his voice small, his lips hardly moving.

"So you knew from the beginning he was involved." Salter had lots of time. He wanted to stay close to Hodek until he knew everything.

"Not at first," Hodek said. "I had never heard of Fisher or Hof when this film started. I left Czechoslovakia in 1968."

"When did you hear?"

"When you started checking up on me in Prague. You remember when Paul was mugged, I told you in Jack's office that we always know when someone is checking up on us."

"I remember."

"I have friends there still, a few. And in West Germany. When your secret service checked up on me, they let me know. I got a call from—from wherever they are, and then I checked up myself." Hodek's words sounded dead, overrehearsed. He had had this conversation with himself a hundred times. "I asked them to find out anything that could connect with the people on the film. I told them the names, and they came back right away with Fisher, and they told me about Jiri Hof. When did you work it out?"

"Yesterday."

"How?"

"I read the article again. In the background stuff Fisher wrote about Hof he mentioned that Hof wanted to marry but it wasn't possible just then. So I wondered who his girlfriend was. After you did, I guess. Then I remembered a couple of other things and realized I had been stumbling over her all the time. Her or her bag," he added. "I never believed she tried to seduce you, Josef. I thought you got rid of her because she'd found out something that would soon tell her that you were the saboteur."

"What was it you remembered?"

"She went out with someone for dinner one night and ate colored food, she said. It connected up with a place called Ron and Tony's, where Fisher had dinner. Did she have an affair with the guy before she killed him?"

"I don't think so. He wanted to seduce her, so he took her out to dinner several times."

"How did she get him to keep their meetings secret?"

"She was supposed to be Sherriff's mistress. Fisher enjoyed being her secret lover. Are you sure she killed him?"

"Fairly. Fisher let her in through the fire escape. Part of the game, I guess."

"She did not want to be seen with him in public. Because of Sherriff, she told him. Her job might be at stake. All of that was true, too."

"That had me wondering. It's hard to figure even a conspirator like Fisher letting someone up the back stairs except a woman."

"But not necessarily Helena." Hodek turned and looked at Salter for the first time.

"No. I thought Fisher didn't want to let the word get back to L.A. that he had been entertaining a woman in his room."

"That would be true, too. That would make it easier for her, of course. If you are right about Helena."

"Did she pull all that stuff—the fire alarms, the swastikas?"

"Somebody did."

Salter realized that Hodek had perceived a gap in Salter's knowledge or certainty and moved quickly to close it. "You helped her. You knew about Hof."

Hodek was silent.

"You switched the film. I found it, Josef. I found the film. It's in the car here now. I found it in the linen closet where you stashed it. You got there early, let the air out of your own tire, and later you stashed the blank film. Neat. But you already told me no one else on the crew could have done it without you knowing. Only you."

Hodek seemed to shrug.

"It threw me off for a while. I suspected you, but I couldn't understand why you were still trying to wreck the film after Fisher's death. I thought maybe Fisher's death wasn't connected, that it was an accident. But I couldn't believe it, so I looked for another reason, maybe another killer. That was when I realized the film incident wasn't connected with Fisher's death but with Helena's being fired, to make it look like she was in the clear. Where is she now?''

Hodek sighed.

''Josef, in those restaurants they went to, Fisher looked like an ordinary upscale patron; they couldn't identify him. But Helena didn't. When I go back to Ron and Tony's with her picture, they'll remember her. I think one of the other places might, too. A case like this, you can't do a thing until you suspect someone; then, if you're right, it's easy. So why waste my time? Sure there are things I don't understand—most of all, your part. So tell me.''

After a long time, Josef spoke, quietly, but with a tone of absolute truth, his decision made. ''I'll tell you what I think might have happened. Here is a girl looking to be married. All right, let us suppose it is Helena. Then, because of some writer's article, she might never see her fiancé again.''

''Why? He only got eight months. Why couldn't she wait for him?''

''I'll tell you. Let me continue. Then she hears that this writer is in Toronto, making a film, so she comes here—she lives in Vancouver—to get her revenge. This writer has a lot of time and money and reputation sunk in the film, so she tries to wreck the film. Then the investigation goes to Prague, clumsily, Charlie, and someone on the set who knows nothing of all this hears he is being investigated, and he does his own investigating and realizes, before the police do, I'm sorry, Charlie, who they are really looking for. She is clever, but he knows they will catch up to her eventually and she will be deported, and he feels sorry for her. The police are slow, but there is a man on the job who calls himself a police adviser, and he is not stupid. So this other man on the set tells the girl to stop and he will try to cover her up, but she is determined. Because now she has met the writer.

"At first, she is very fair. She lets him date her so they can talk about his experiences in Czechoslovakia. She goes to his room. She wants him to know what he has done, that's all. He says it crossed his mind that he wouldn't be doing Jiri any good. *Crossed his mind, Charlie*. Perhaps, she says, he should not have written the article, and perhaps he is sorry. He says a writer has to use any material that comes to hand. Even if it will destroy someone? she asks. The writer is sorry about that, he says, but it was too good a story.

"Then quite by the way he tells her how happy he is about the sabotage, because if the film is taken away from Jack, then they will give it to him to finish. So instead of hurting him, getting her own back, she has been playing into his hands all the time. That is too much for her. The knife is handy. It is a crime of passion, Charlie."

"He doesn't know who she is?" Salter asked.

"Not until she tells him."

"You knew she might do something like this."

"Not too fast, please. Her friend on the set thinks that she will be caught for trying to sabotage the film, so he makes it harder for the police by doing a couple of things himself, things she couldn't have done."

"Like damaging his own sound recorder?"

"This girl is in real trouble. Perhaps to waste two hours to repair a sound machine will satisfy her and she will go back to Vancouver. It's a big price, but there is enough time left to finish."

"What about the film? That can of film cost a lot of money to make."

"The girl will be deported if she is caught. There was time to finish the film, or find it. So she is fired, and then the film disappears, an incident that she could not have done."

"You had to do that?"

"This man on the set tried to persuade her to go away when he realized who she was and he would cover for her, but she would not go. Yes. Then Fisher is killed, and he knows he is too late, but it is even more important that she get fired and a bit more sabotage happen." Hodek was exhausted now, beyond fright.

"Where is she now?"

"Not in Canada, I think. If she is wise, she will have gone to Frankfurt and then back to her own country."

"What'll happen to her there?"

"She might spend some time being rehabilitated. Not very nice, but things are changing quickly now, and perhaps in a few months, a year or two, she will be able to leave. So one day she will be able to come back to Canada."

"No."

"Why not?" Hodek became passionate. "The police do not have enough evidence to extradite her. We are just talking now."

"We know she was seeing Fisher."

"Do you? You haven't shown her picture to the restaurant yet. All you have is a little remark about colored food."

"I'll show the picture around. She was with him the night he was killed. And everything in the forensic lab from the hotel room will connect her to him."

"Have you found anyone who saw them together yet?"

"The hotel clerk says he came home alone. But then I think Fisher let her up the back stairs."

"Helena? Or someone else. Ask me where Helena was on Sunday night. Please. Ask me."

"Okay. Where was she?"

"She was with us, remember? My wife and me. She called us to see if she could come and talk about going home. As you know, things have been getting so liberal in her country that she decided to go home. When we saw Helena on Sunday night, she was cheerful and bright."

"Does she intend to wait for her boyfriend to get out of jail? Live happily ever after? Is he out already, under the new regime?"

"She will never be very happy, Charlie. Jiri Hof never came out of jail. He was transferred to a labor camp, then to a mine, and then he disappeared. The records are lost. He's dead, of course."

"Jesus." Salter rolled down the car window. "Were they really engaged?" he asked when the silence had gone on too long.

"They must have been in love, Charlie. Look what she's done."

Salter tried to carry on being a Toronto cop. "We could find her in Frankfurt, before she crosses the border."

"Oh, it's too late for that, I think. But what would happen if you did? I don't think you could extradite her just to ask her some questions. If the Romanian police will do that for you, you will find no more than you know now."

"The knife came from the set."

"Fisher picked it up as a souvenir. She did not go to his room to kill him."

Salter considered his options.

Josef continued, his voice thin and cracking. "If you accused her, at least everyone would know why she did it. But the price is too high."

"Whatever happens, she should not try to come back. Ever. The file will stay open, and someone one day will get an idea, and she might pay the price. The technicians took away plenty of evidence from the room; all they need is someone to match it to. And I think maybe other people who were involved would pay a price. Are they prepared to do that? She may be beyond reach, but you're here. You, Josef. Prison, then expulsion. You are taking a hell of a chance. Do you like it here?"

Hodek's normally papery skin had acquired the dull glaze of wet putty. "This is my home. But what could I do? I have avoided taking chances all my life, but this was one I had to take. The girl didn't know what she was doing, but she will still end up in prison here or in a psychiatric ward. What good is that?"

Salter said, "She shouldn't try to come back, this girl."

"If she thinks about that, she will realize it. Her friends will tell her."

Salter knew he was talking to give himself room to think. It would be very hard to prove. Fisher had let someone into his room. He had been killed by a dagger from the set. As Hodek had reminded him, Fisher might have taken the dagger himself for a souvenir.

Hodek had done a lot of thinking. He was prepared to swear that Helena was absolutely composed on Sunday night when she appeared at their house. Salter wondered at what point Josef had made his own decision, one that could wreck his own life. Salter reminded himself that he had a witness—Sherriff—who had seen Fisher arrive home alone.

He abandoned the pretext that they were talking hypothetically. "Did Helena see Sherriff parked outside the hotel?"

"I would think so. She would know his car."

The point of Salter's question had been to see if Hodek was surprised at the introduction of Sherriff's name. So Helena had seen Sherriff before he saw her, and she hadn't been noticed by the devout cabdriver, either. If they did manage to get to her in Romania, her story would be simple and solid. She had visited Hodek, ten miles from where Fisher had been killed.

Now Salter considered the film. It was still missing. Only Josef and he knew that it had been put in the linen closet and that the flat tire was an effective decoy to divert the search. There were some other details, though.

"Who beat up Diamond?" Salter asked.

Now, for the first time, Hodek smiled. "Who tried to beat up Diamond? A young Czech boy being gallant. A hockey player. He was in love with Helena, who probably told him that Diamond had tried to seduce her. Perhaps the same one who made the phone calls."

"Where is he now?"

"Oh, he could be anywhere. There is a Czech community in Vancouver. What does it matter?"

Salter said, "Are you going to stay here?"

"I told you, it is a beautiful country. This is my home, and I don't want to move. I would like to build a cottage, like Mr. Orliff."

"Get out of the car now. No, don't let's shake hands. I don't know what I'm going to do next."

Hodek got out, and Salter watched as he walked to his car, leaned on it, and turned, his mouth open, struggling for breath, it looked like. Then he wrapped his arms around himself and took four or five deep breaths. He looked as if he were going to throw up, but he held on to himself and opened the car door and sat down. After five minutes his lights came on, and he drove slowly toward the exit.

Salter watched him go, then followed him along Queen's Quay, up Bay Street, until Hodek turned right on Gerrard. There wasn't much traffic. He would be all right now.

THE NEXT MORNING, Salter called Crabtree. "I think we've found your film," he said. "Guy just called in anonymously and told us it's on the porch of that house you rented in Oakville. He wouldn't tell us his name. Some kind of European accent. I'm sending a car out to pick it up."

TWENTY-ONE

THE REPORT he prepared was simple enough. It ruled out the possibility of any right-wing activity. It detailed the sabotage acts and demonstrated that no single person could have committed them, except someone with such a minor position that they would be impossible to find. The stealing and returning of the can of film was the biggest puzzle. Now that the incidents had stopped, there was little chance of finding the culprit.

Then he wrote a second report, on Fisher. His death was being investigated by Homicide because together they had been unable to find any connection with the film. The evidence pointed to his having let someone in through the back door. It was not known where he had had dinner that night. He had arrived home early, about ten o'clock. The dagger came from the set, but could have been taken by the victim much earlier and used by the killer in the course of an argument. The only other possibility (and this only because at one time Fisher was a possible suspect in the sabotage incidents) was that Fisher was involved with someone in those incidents, someone who came to get paid. (Here Salter carefully described Fisher's connection with Porter Williams as an instance of Fisher's character.)

Finally, he removed from the file the charge slips from the restaurants and put them in his pocket. Anyone going over his tracks would find that the charge slips had disappeared somewhere between Salter's office and Burnley's file. It happened all the time.

When he was finished, he wrote a formal note to Burnley, as they had agreed, describing his investigation of a possible Czech connection in such a way that indicated that he thought it was unlikely. Burnley could read a different emphasis when he came to his own dead end.

THEY WERE SITTING three rows from the front: Salter, Annie, his father, May (his father's companion), Henry Vigor, and Ranovic.

Eight girls in tutus trotted across the stage, each with head bent and a hand across the brow. When they had all arrived, they turned and went through a series of maneuvers like the police motorcycle team, coming to a halt in line abreast, peering, hands shielding their eyes, offstage. Seth and his friend appeared and leaped about for a while before noticing the girls. Then Seth jumped into the air and ran at one of the girls, who ran away in a kind of swooping, dive-bombing motion, Seth following. A courting dance followed, which ended when Seth threw the girl away and went back to chat with his friend. Now the friend ran at another girl and repeated Seth's performance. After a while, they had chased four girls each, and then a ninth girl appeared, somewhat taller than the others and wearing a black tutu. She danced frenziedly with each of the boys in turn until the boys fell exhausted to the floor. Then the eight girls picked up Seth and his friend and carried them offstage while the girl in black danced by herself for a bit and then shuddered for a long time, with her arms in the air, as the curtain came down.

"Good boy," Salter's father shouted. "Good boy, Seth."

Now they had to wait. Now Maisie Flint, the director of the troupe Seth wanted to join, would decide his fate on the basis of what she had seen. It had been arranged that Seth would meet them in the Harbourfront restaurant after his interview, where, win or lose, they would all celebrate.

On the way over Henry Vigor drew Salter ahead of the group. "Don't get your hopes up, Charlie. I don't think your son is meant to be a dancer."

"I thought he was terrific."

"He was. On the other hand, he was no good at all."

There was no opportunity to warn Annie or the others, and Salter waited in some fear for Seth to arrive. When he did, he was accompanied by a very pretty girl, one of the ones he had chased about onstage, and his friend Sammy Frier. There was no way for Salter to arrange a soft landing if Vigor was right. It was Seth's evening. When they were all settled, Seth raised Sammy's hand. "Drink to the champ," he said. "Maisie says he's in."

After a minute, Salter said, "That it, Seth?"

Seth nodded.

"What a bloody rotten shame," Salter's father said, staring at Sammy with hostility.

"You want to go home?" Annie asked.

"Oh, no. I'm starving. So is Cathy." He put his arm around the girl's neck. "And we have to be Sammy's family. Help him celebrate. They couldn't come."

The extraordinary thing was that in a very little time there were three conversations going, and when they

left, everyone seemed cheerful. It was like a wake, a
real wake.

SALTER SAID, "Believe it or not, I feel as bad as you
do. Once I got used to the idea, I was all for Seth to do
well. It feels like the time I'd set my heart on hockey
and found out I wasn't even good enough for the Flin
Flon Bombers. The difference is that I could still play
on a factory team once I was used to the idea. But the
kid can't dance anymore, can he? I'm as sorry as you
are."

Annie put her book aside and turned off the light.
"Don't worry about me. I'm relieved."

"You're what?"

"I'm glad. I knew he wasn't any Nijinsky, but I
couldn't see any harm in letting him find out for himself. He needed our support, and you did well. But I'm
glad he's as bad as he is. If Sammy Frier is good
enough, he'll get to be principal dancer with the Sas-
katoon ballet. He'll be in constant pain from dancing
and rehearsing eight or twelve hours a day. He'll earn
four hundred a week for thirty-six weeks and have to
support himself for the other sixteen. Below the minimum wage."

"That's worse than the Flin Flon Bombers."

"It's a life of poverty—literally—and then at thirty
you become a stagehand. So when I realized he was no
Nijinsky, I prayed that he would be as bad as he apparently is."

"You didn't say a word about all this."

Annie was silent.

"So it's back to school for him. Then what?"

"I'll give you one guess."

"What?"

"Acting. Didn't you realize how much he was infected by Henry? I asked Henry. He thinks we should let him try. Trainable, his word was. He thinks Seth is trainable."

"Christ, and then we'll have to go through all this again?"

"It's not so black and white. He can stay in school, go to university while he finds out if he has any talent. It's more manageable."

"I see. You'll keep me in touch, will you?"

"Go to sleep, Charlie."

D · A · T · E

WITH A DEAD

DOCTOR

TONI · BRILL

Midge Cohen's mother has fixed her up again. What would it hurt to meet this nice Jewish doctor, a urologist even, and give him a try, she insists.

But all Dr. Leon Skripnik wants from Midge, an erstwhile Russian scholar, is a translation of a letter he's received from the old country. To get rid of him she agrees to his request. The next morning, he's found dead.

"An engaging first novel. A warm, observant, breezy talent is evident here."

—*Kirkus Reviews*

COFFIN UNDERGROUND

First Time in Paperback

Gwendoline Butler

FOR THE TWISTED AND TALENTED, MURDER IS A GAME

Scotland Yard Chief Superintendent John Coffin is properly skeptical of the evil reputation of the house at No. 22, Church Row. True, the house has seen violent death over the centuries. None of it suspicious. Until now. Malcolm Kincaid, student. Bill Egan, recidivist. Terry Place, villain. Edward, Irene and Nona Pitt, victims. Phyllis Henley, policewoman. Why have they died?

Coffin suspects something more than a haunted house. He sees a human, complex web of relationships, interlocking and interacting in a way he can't yet fathom, and in which people get caught up and destroyed—as they play into the game of a very clever killer.

"...appealing hero ... a gripping tale of sinister fantasy role-playing and bloody murder, sure to be relished."   —*Booklist*

A GINNY TRASK AND FRANK CARVER MYSTERY

First
Time in
Paperback

COLD TRACKS

Lee Wallingford

BLOOD LEAVES A DEADLY TRAIL

Tired of the violence of big-city crime, former narcotics agent Frank Carver trades the streets of Seattle for the penny-ante stuff of Oregon's Neskanie National Forest. Work is wonderfully, refreshingly dull for the forest's new law-enforcement officer. No shootings. No bodies. No murders.

Until the corpse of Nino Alvarez, an immigrant worker, is found in the woods by fire dispatcher Ginny Trask.

"Skillful debut. This intriguing pair of detectives—a burned-out cop and a beautiful young widow—promise future entertaining reading."

—*Publishers Weekly*

OTHER PEOPLE'S HOUSES

SUSAN ROGERS COOPER

In Prophesy County, Oklahoma, the unlikely event of a homicide is coupled with the likely event that if one occurs, the victim is somebody everybody knows....

And everybody knows nice bank teller Lois Bell who, along with her husband and three kids, dies of accidental carbon monoxide poisoning. But things just aren't sitting right with chief deputy Milton Kovak. Why were the victims' backgrounds completely untraceable? And why was the federal government butting its nose in the case?

"Milt Kovak tells his story with a voice that's as comforting as a rocking chair and as salty as a fisherman."

—*Houston Chronicle*

THE UNDERGROUND STREAM

First Time in Paperback

VELDA JOHNSTON

AN OLD HOUSE WITH ... EVEN OLDER SECRETS

For twenty-four years, Gail Loring has fought both her fear of the alcoholic haze in which the women of her family have lived *and* the haunting images of a man—her great-great-great-grandfather—called the Monster of Monroe Street.

Now Gail can run no longer. At her ancestral home in the summer resort town of Hampton Harbor, she vows to confront the past. She finds herself stepping back into the stream of time. She is Martha Fitzwilliam, a young wife and mother who lived here more than a hundred and fifty years ago. Gail shares Martha's secrets ... and feels her terror. A terror she must pursue to its ultimate act of shattering violence....

"The vicissitudes of time and place are skillfully evoked in this eerie and often dream-like novel." —*Publishers Weekly*